Tuf held up a ha

He grinned and Cheyenne's heart hammered wildly. Oh, he was good. But as tempting as he was, she still had to say no. Even though it had been more than ten years, they still weren't right for each other. They had too much baggage and heartache to deal with.

Then Tuf did something unexpected. He reached across the table and gently ran one long finger across her freckles. He'd never touched her before, and a sea of emotions swamped her, emotions she'd just sworn she didn't have. Why was she suddenly hot all over and why did she have the urge to giggle?

"In grade school, I thought your freckles were cute. I actually tried to count them one time. You frowned at me so I had to stop counting. I like the freckles."

Was he for real?

"I'd really like it if we could be friends. Do you think that's possible?"

No. No. No!

But the word that slipped from Cheyenne's lips was "Yes."

Dear Reader,

Tomas: Cowboy Homecoming is the last book in the Harts of the Rodeo continuity series. Please don't miss the other five books: *Aidan: Loyal Cowboy* by Cathy McDavid, *Colton: Rodeo Cowboy* by C.J. Carmichael, *Duke: Deputy Cowboy* by Roz Denny Fox, *Austin: Second Chance Cowboy* by Shelley Galloway and *Beau: Cowboy Protector* by Marin Thomas. I'm excited to be a part of this project and to work with these talented authors. I grew up in rural Texas and rodeo was a big thing and lots of fun. I never thought about what went on behind the scenes. After researching this book, I now know more about rodeos and cowboys and cowgirls than I ever thought I would.

My character Tomas, nicknamed Tuf, is the youngest of the Hart family. As a kid he was always trying to prove he was as tough as his older brothers and cousins. When his dad passed away, he joined the marines to find his own way in life. He returns home a hero, but scarred. The first person he meets is Cheyenne Sundell, a girl he had a crush on in high school. But Cheyenne is dealing with her own kind of pain. Her deceased marine husband committed suicide. It was a challenge to pull together two deeply scarred characters against the backdrop of the rodeo. I hope their love story is as real to you as it was to me.

So saddle up. We're going to a rodeo—and all the way to the National Finals Rodeo in Las Vegas, Nevada, for the ride of your life on a black stallion named Midnight. Don't forget your hat and boots.

With love and thanks,

Linda Warren

It's always a pleasure to hear from readers. You can email me at Lw1508@aol.com or write me at P.O. Box 5182, Bryan, TX 77805. I will answer your letters as soon as I can. Or visit my website at www.LindaWarren.net or join me on Facebook or on Twitter, @texauthor.

Tomas: Cowboy Homecoming

LINDA WARREN

Recycling programs for this product may not exist in your area.

ISBN-13: 978-0-373-75433-5

TOMAS: COWBOY HOMECOMING

This edition published by arrangement with Harlequin Books S.A.

For questions and comments about the quality of this book, please contact us at CustomerService@Harlequin.com.

www.Harlequin.com

Printed in U.S.A.

ABOUT THE AUTHOR

RITA® Award nominated and award-winning author Linda Warren has written thirty-one books for Harlequin, including stories for the Superromance, American Romance and Everlasting Love lines. Drawing upon her years of growing up on a farm/ranch in Texas, she writes about sexy heroes, feisty heroines and broken families with an emotional punch—all set against the backdrop of Texas. When she's not writing or at the mall, she's sitting on her patio with her husband watching the wildlife and plotting her next book. Visit her website at www.LindaWarren.net.

Books by Linda Warren

HARLEQUIN AMERICAN ROMANCE

1042—THE CHRISTMAS CRADLE
1089—CHRISTMAS, TEXAS STYLE
"Merry Texmas"
1102—THE COWBOY'S RETURN
1151—ONCE A COWBOY
1226—TEXAS HEIR
1249—THE SHERIFF OF HORSESHOE, TEXAS

HARLEQUIN SUPERROMANCE

1167—A BABY BY CHRISTMAS
1121—THE RIGHT WOMAN
1250—FORGOTTEN SON
1314—ALL ROADS LEAD TO TEXAS
1354—SON OF TEXAS
1375—THE BAD SON
1440—ADOPTED SON
1470—TEXAS BLUFF
1499—ALWAYS A MOTHER
1574—CAITLYN'S PRIZE*
1592—MADISON'S CHILDREN*
1610—SKYLAR'S OUTLAW*
1723—THE TEXAN'S SECRET**
1735—THE TEXAN'S BRIDE**
1747—THE TEXAN'S CHRISTMAS**

*The Belles of Texas
**The Hardin Boys

To my wonderful editor, Kathleen Scheibling,
for creating the Harts of the Rodeo and giving us such interesting characters to develop.
And a temperamental black stallion to tame.

To Johanna Raisanen for editing the books to make them the best they could be.

To the men and women in our military. Thank you.

Acknowledgments

Thanks to all the people who answered my many questions about rodeo, especially Catherine Laycraft from the Calgary Stampede. And a special thanks to Rogenna for sharing her knowledge of the military. And for all the info available on the internet about rodeo and PTSD.

All errors are strictly mine.

Chapter One

Home to Thunder Ranch.

In a coffin.

The only way Marine Staff Sergeant Tomas "Tuf" Hart ever saw himself returning to the place of his birth from the battlefields of Afghanistan was in a pine box.

Draped with an American flag.

Every time his unit engaged the enemy, bullets whizzed past him as mortar fire exploded in his ears. Two of his buddies died not twelve feet from him, but he'd been spared. Unscathed. Except for the invisible wounds on his soul that would be with him a lifetime. He'd seen too many innocent women and children killed for them not to.

But that was behind him and he was ready to see his family again. Though he'd been out of the Marine Corps two years, he hadn't been home. Explaining that wasn't going to be easy, but talking about the war was something he didn't do, and he hoped his family respected that.

The sleepy town of Roundup, Montana, nestled in the pine-clad valley of the Bull Mountains. The town got its name because the valley near the Musselshell River was a natural place for ranchers to round up their cattle.

It was three days after Christmas and the town was quiet as he drove down a snow-covered Main Street, tire-track trails visible in the slush. Red-and-green decorations still fluttered from every building. Familiar storefronts. He noticed a redbrick building with black trim—Number 1 Diner. That was new, but otherwise the place was the same—his hometown.

He left town and turned south, taking the county road leading to the ranch. A light snow began to fall and he flipped on the windshield wipers. As he rounded a corner, he saw a little girl about four or five walking on the side of the road. She wore a heavy purple coat with a fur-lined hood, but the hood wasn't over her head. Flakes of snow clung to her red hair, gathered into a ponytail, as she purposefully marched forward in snow boots.

A flashback hit him. He hadn't had one in months. He could see the little girl in Afghanistan, hear the rapid spatter of gunfire, the shouts, the screams and then an unholy silence. Stopping the truck in the middle of the road, he gripped the steering wheel with clammy hands. He took a quick breath and closed his eyes, forcing happier memories into his mind as his counselor had taught him.

He was fishing on Thunder Creek with his dad. "Come on, boy. The big ones bite early. Throw your line next to that old stump." Tuf would grin and throw the line where his father had showed him.

"That's my boy."

He opened his eyes as the flashback ebbed away. The little girl trekked forward in the snow, a good distance from him now. He eased the truck closer and got out.

What was she doing out here all alone? Buddy Wright's was the closest place, and he didn't have any young kids Tuf knew about.

"Hey," he called, but the girl ignored him. She did move farther into the ditch, though. His boots slipped and slid on the snow-slick blacktop, but he made it to her without falling on his ass. "Hey, what are you doing out here?"

The little girl frowned up at him, her green eyes narrowed. "I'm not 'posed to talk to strangers."

"Listen..."

"Sadie! Sadie!" a frantic voice called, and Tuf turned his head to see a woman running toward them. She was dressed in a denim skirt, brown boots, a suede vest and a white blouse. No coat. And the temperature was below freezing. Her deep red hair, the color of cinnamon, glistened with snow.

Cheyenne Wright.

He'd know her anywhere.

Even though she was a year younger, he'd had a huge crush on her in high school. Since he was a bareback rider and she was a barrel racer, he saw her often at rodeos. He had asked her out twice and she'd said no both times. Figuring third time's a charm, he'd asked again and got the same answer. Puzzled and frustrated he'd asked why. Her response was "I don't like you, Tuf Hart."

That had dented his puffed-up seventeen-year-old ego. He didn't get it. He was reasonably good-looking, well liked by everyone in school and he had his own pickup. Back then that was a sure thing to get a date. Not with Cheyenne. But he didn't think it to death because he was aware the Hart and Wright families didn't get along.

Buddy was an alcoholic and had served time in prison for stealing cattle. John Hart hadn't wanted the man on his property. So Tuf, as teenage boys are known to do, moved on. He never forgot the shy, untouchable Cheyenne, though.

Since he was twenty-eight, she had to be about twenty-seven now, and she still looked the same with dark red hair and green eyes. And a slim curved body he'd spent many nights dreaming about.

She squatted and pulled the child into her arms. At that point, Tuf noticed an identical little girl running to catch up to Cheyenne. *Twins.* This one had the hood over her head and was bundled up tight in a pink winter coat.

"Mommy," the second twin cried.

"It's all right, Sammie," Cheyenne said in a soothing, soft voice. "I found Sadie." Cheyenne brushed the snow from Sadie's hair and covered it with the hood, securing it with the drawstring. Her fingers shook from the cold as she touched Sadie's red cheeks. "I've been looking all over for you. What are you doing out here?"

"I'd like to know that, too."

Cheyenne stood, holding on to the girls' hands. Her eyes narrowed much as her daughter's had. The sparkling green eyes of the cool, aloof Cheyenne from high school were gone. Now he saw only disillusionment in their depths. A look he knew well. He saw it every morning when he looked in the mirror. What had happened to her life?

"I'll take care of my daughter," she replied, as cool as the snowflakes falling on her hair.

"I hope you do. I could have hit her. Anyone driving on this road could have, and then two lives would have been changed forever."

"I'm sorry if she disturbed…your drive."

He heard the derision in her voice and he relented a little. "It's dangerous out here."

"I'm aware of that." She looked down at her daughters and ignored him, much as she had in high school. "Let's go home where it's warm." They walked away, Cheyenne holding the girls' hands.

"I didn't talk to him, Mommy, 'cause he's a stranger," Sadie said.

"Good, baby."

Cheyenne started to run and the girls followed suit. Sadie glanced back at him as they disappeared into the Wrights' driveway.

Tuf pulled his sheep-lined jacket tighter around him to block the chill of a Montana December.

Welcome home, Tuf.

Some things just never changed. Cheyenne still didn't like him.

CHEYENNE USHERED THE GIRLS into the living room and sat them down by the fire. For a moment she let her chilled body soak up the warmth. When she stopped trembling, she hurried to the bathroom for a towel. Rushing back, she removed the girls' new Christmas coats and dried Sadie's hair and face, as well as her own. Her clothes were damp and she needed to change, but she had to talk to Sadie first.

She sat between them. "Sadie, baby, why do you keep running away?"

Sadie shrugged.

Cheyenne brushed back one of Sadie's flyaway curls. "Mommy is worried. Please stop this."

Sammie crawled into her lap. "I won't run away, Mommy."

She kissed Sammie's warm cheek. Their father's death had affected the girls so differently. Sammie clung to her while Sadie was defiant and seemed determined to get away from her. Cheyenne was at her wit's end trying to get Sadie to talk about what was bothering her.

Gathering the girls close, she whispered, "I love you guys."

"I love you, too, Mommy." Sammie was quick to say the words.

Fat tears rolled from Sadie's eyes. "I…I…" she blubbered.

Cheyenne held her tighter, feeling hopeless. Why couldn't she help her child? She smoothed Sadie's hair and kissed her forehead. "You love Mommy?"

Sadie nodded and Cheyenne held her daughters, wondering how she was ever going to reach Sadie. The fire crackled with renewed warmth, and she leaned against her dad's recliner holding the two most important people in the world to her. They snuggled against her.

Cheyenne's body was so cold she didn't think she'd ever get warm again. The fear in her slowly subsided. They'd been in town and on the way home when Sammie suddenly had to go to the bathroom. Running into the house, she'd turned on the TV for Sadie and helped Sammie out of her coat. When they'd come out of the bathroom, Sadie was gone. Cheyenne was frantic, calling and calling for Sadie.

It wasn't the first time Sadie had disappeared, and Cheyenne had tried to breathe past the fear. But Sadie wasn't in the yard or at the barn. Sammie trailed behind her crying. Cheyenne made her go back into the house for her coat. It was cold. The only place left was the road, and it had started to snow again.

When she saw a truck stopped and a man talking to her child, real terror had leaped into her throat. She had to do better than this.

And the man had turned out to be Tuf Hart, the last person she'd thought she would ever see again. She was too worried about Sadie to give him much thought. He'd changed, but she still knew who he was. He was the only man who ever made her nervous and excited at the same time. One thing was clear, though: the skinny, affable boy from school had returned a man, with broad shoulders and a muscled body that was toned from rigorous training. She knew that from her marine husband, Ryan. He'd hated the training, but Tuf seemed to have flourished in it.

Tuf is home.

His family would be so relieved. He'd called his mom two years ago to let her know he was out of the marines and okay. After that, there'd been no word until his cousin Beau had seen him at a rodeo in November. Tuf still didn't come home, though. The family was worried. Understandably so. Beau had assured the family that Tuf looked fine. Cheyenne could attest to that. Tuf Hart looked very fine. Yet different somehow. Being a marine changed men. It had changed Ryan and not for the better. Mentally it had destroyed him. And their marriage.

The front door opened and her dad came in after wiping his boots on the mat. He removed his hat and coat, hooking them on the wrought-iron coatrack. Tall and lean with a thatch of gray hair, Buddy Wright's rugged, lined face showed a life of too much alcohol and too many days on the wrong side of the law.

Cheyenne thought she'd never return to Roundup. As a young girl, her dream was to leave and get far away from her alcoholic father. He'd caused her and her brother, Austin, so much heartache. Yet when she was at her lowest, she'd come home to the only parent she had.

He'd finally stopped drinking and gotten his life together. It couldn't have happened at a better time for both his children. Austin had married Dinah Hart, and the Wrights were now included in the Hart family circle. It was a what's-wrong-with-this-picture type thing. When John Hart was alive, he made it clear Buddy was not welcome at Thunder Ranch. That was the main reason she would never go out with Tuf. The Harts were a prominent family and the Wrights were from the wrong side of the tracks. She would not expose her wounded pride to the Harts, especially Tuf.

"I thought you were coming to the celebration," her dad said.

"I was, but—" She got to her feet and flipped on the TV. The girls scurried to sit in front of it. "Sadie ran away again."

"Again?" Her father followed her into the kitchen and watched as she made coffee. "I wondered what had happened. Leah was asking about you, and Jill wanted to know when the twins were coming, so I thought I'd better come check."

"Tuf Hart found her walking in the ditch by the road."

"Tuf?" One of her father's shaggy gray eyebrows rose as she placed a cup of hot coffee in front of him. "Are you sure?"

"Yes, Dad. I know Tuf Hart." She stirred milk and sugar into her coffee and sat at the table with him. "He's changed, though. He's not that laughing, fun-loving kid anymore. He seems so serious now."

"War does that to a man." Her father took a sip of his hot coffee, making that face he always made when he took the first taste. That oh-I-needed-this look. He sat the mug down. "The family must not know he's coming or Sarah would have been so excited. He must be planning a surprise visit."

She toyed with her cup. "I thought of calling Dinah, but if Tuf wants to surprise them, that's his business. I'm not getting involved."

"Wise decision." Her dad frowned. "Wonder where he's been for two years."

"Dinah thinks he was wounded and in a navy hospital somewhere recovering and didn't want the family to worry."

"Did he look like he'd been wounded?"

"He seemed okay."

"He'll have some questions to answer, but like you said, it's none of our business."

"No."

Her father eyed her. "So you're not going to the party?"

"I'm not rewarding Sadie with fun time. I have to start disciplining her." And that would just about kill Cheyenne. "I'm going to fix them something to eat and put Sammie to bed. Then Sadie and I are going to have a talk. She'll shrug and start crying like always. Honestly, Dad, I don't know what to do anymore."

He patted her hand on the table. "Just love her."

She nodded and got to her feet. "I imagine there's a lot of celebrating going on at Thunder Ranch right about now. I hope for Tuf's sake everyone is glad to see him."

"Sarah will be happy to see her youngest child."

"But what about the rest of the family? The ones who have been struggling to save John Hart's legacy?" Cheyenne took their cups to the sink. "I'm glad we're not there. This is family time."

"You bet. I'm going to check on the horses." He ambled back into the living room to get his hat and coat.

Tuf Hart was home and that didn't mean a thing to her. She planned to stay away from him, just as she had as a teenager.

TUF TURNED ONTO THUNDER ROAD that led to the ranch. He stopped the truck once again and stared. The big two-story house he'd grown up in was lit up like a Christmas tree, and the driveway was full of parked trucks and cars. What was going on? His mom always had Christmas on Christmas day, so they couldn't be celebrating the holiday.

Not wanting to deal with a crowd, he drove to the barns, parked and got out.

He breathed in the heady scent of the ponderosa pines and saw the snow-covered Bull Mountains in the distance. He was home. No more war. No more killing. No more dying.

It had stopped snowing and the air was fresh and invigorating. Glancing toward the house, he decided to wait a while before making his appearance. An agitated neighing caught his attention and he walked toward the corral attached to the barn. A beautiful black stallion circled the pen. At the sight of Tuf, the horse reared his head and pawed the ground with one hoof.

Tuf leaned on the fence and watched the black horse with the flowing mane. He was magnificent and Tuf wondered what he was doing on Thunder Ranch. The more he watched, the more agitated the horse became, snorting, his nostrils flaring as he pawed the ground. Finally the horse trotted over to a dun mare drinking from a water trough. The mare's rounded belly indicated she was pregnant. The two neighed back and forth and the black horse seemed to calm down.

"Tuf?"

He looked over his shoulder to see Royce, one of the ranch hands, staring at him. "Hey, Royce."

"Man, it is you." Royce vigorously shook his hand. "Your mom's gonna be beside herself. I'll give her a call." Royce reached for his cell.

"No." Tuf stopped him. "I'll surprise her in a minute." He glanced toward the house. "What's going on?"

The other man frowned. "You don't know?"

"What?"

"Beau got married today and your mom threw him and Sierra a big reception."

"What?" He'd seen Beau at a rodeo in November, and he hadn't said anything about getting married, but then, Tuf hadn't given him time to talk. Beau had been full of questions and Tuf couldn't answer them. He wanted to go home but couldn't, and Beau wouldn't understand that. Making a quick exit was all he could do.

"Go on up to the house and join the celebration," Royce urged.

Feeling chilled, Tuf pulled the collar up on his coat, his eyes centering on the black horse, who was watching him as Tuf had watched the horse earlier. "What's the story on the horse?"

Royce leaned on the fence. "That's Midnight. Ain't he a beauty? Your mom and Ace bought him at an auction when his owner died. The foreman mistreated him so he's a little gun-shy, if you know what I mean. His lineage goes back to the great bucking horse Five Minutes to Midnight and they paid a pretty penny for him."

"Yeah. He's prime horseflesh."

"Ace outbid ol' Earl McKinley, and Earl wasn't too happy." Royce shook his head. "Midnight has caused a whole passel of problems. Went missing for a while and upset the whole family. Turned out thieves who were stealing tack left the gate open and Midnight sprinted for freedom. The horse turned up at Buddy Wright's place. That gave everyone pause, but Buddy just patched up the horse's wounds and kept him safe. Ol' Buddy has changed a lot."

Tuf digested that for a minute. It would be nice if the Hart and Wright families could exist in peace. Life was too short for petty grievances.

Royce watched the horse. "Very temperamental and hard to handle, but Ace and Colt are working wonders with him."

"Is he for breeding or bucking?"

"Depends on who you ask. Ace wants to keep breeding him, but Colt's entered him in a few rodeos. Midnight twisted his left knee in November, and the family is at odds on what to do with him now. Ace doesn't want to risk getting him injured again. The family has a lot riding on that black horse." Royce peered at him. "You do know the Harts are in the rodeo contracting business?"

"Mom mentioned that."

"Things have changed since you've been gone."

"Mmm." He'd spent six years fighting in a war-torn country, sometimes sleeping on the ground and living off military-issue food not fit for a dog, but it kept him alive. It was always a celebration to get back to base for real food. He'd almost forgotten what it was like to live in the real world and to enjoy the freedom he'd been fighting for. His adjustment was yet to come.

Midnight reared up on his hind legs, pawing at the air, clearly upset at the stranger eyeing him.

"Calm down," Royce said to the horse, and Midnight trotted back to the dun mare.

"Do you leave him out here all night?"

Royce slapped him on the back. "Man, you have been gone a long time if you've forgotten what Ace is like." Royce pointed to the right of the barn. "See that opening? It goes into Midnight's personal oversize stall. Once the mare goes inside, he'll follow. She has a calming effect on him."

"I noticed."

"Midnight hates being penned up. He likes open spaces. When he injured his knee, we closed the doors and Midnight went crazy. Ace had to sedate him to keep him calm so he wouldn't injure the leg further. That horse is either gonna make or break Thunder Ranch." He held out his hand to Tuf. "Glad to have you home. Go join the celebration and make your mama happy. I'm feeding the pregnant mares, but I'll be up for some grub as soon as I finish."

Tuf nodded and breathed in the crisp air off Bull Mountains. Time to face the family, but he couldn't take his eyes off Midnight, who continued to circle the pen.

"I've dreamed of riding a horse like you all my life," he muttered under his breath.

Midnight flung his head and stomped his hoof again in protest as if he understood every word.

"Tomas. Tomas. Tomas!"

Only one person called him that. His mother. Damn! Royce had called. He turned around as his mother flew across the yard in a dress and heels. At the sight of her silver hair and smiling face, his heart thumped against his ribs. Oh, how he'd missed his mom.

How did he explain the past two years?

Chapter Two

"Tomas!" His mom grabbed him in a bear hug. He held on with arms that felt weak, but he was buffeted by a strength he couldn't describe. Being over six feet, he leaned down so she could kiss his cheek. He'd started doing that when he was about fourteen.

Sarah stroked his face and then ran her hands over his shoulders, arms and chest, much like when he was younger and a horse would buck him into the dirt. "Are you hurt? Are you okay?"

"I'm fine, Mom." The family stood behind her all dressed in their Sunday best. Some of the faces he didn't recognize. The guys were in pressed jeans, pristine Western white shirts with bolo ties. The women were in dresses or suits. Before he could see anything else, his brothers, Aidan and Colton, nicknamed Ace and Colt, barreled into him with fierce hugs, and then twin cousins Beau and Duke and Uncle Josh. He'd missed this connection to family.

Someone grabbed his arm and jerked him around. His sister Dinah's fiery hazel eyes flashed up at him. "Where have you been? You've had us all worried sick."

"Hey, sis." He reached for her and lifted her off her feet into a tight embrace.

"Be careful. She's pregnant," Sarah warned.

"Oh." Tuf eased her to the ground.

Dinah laughed. "Get that look off your face. I'm respectably married." She pulled a guy forward. "This is my husband, Austin. You remember him?"

Austin Wright. His sister had married Austin Wright, Cheyenne's brother. How did that happen?

Before he could find an answer, his mother linked her arm through his. "Let's go to the house. It's cold out here. We have a lot to celebrate. My baby is home."

Baby. Usually when she called him that, it would cause sparks of resentment to flash inside him. Thank God he had finally outgrown that reaction.

Dinah also linked her arm through his, and they made their way into the house through the spacious, homey kitchen to the great room. He barely had time to remove his hat. People milled around him. To the right was a long buffet table laden with prime rib and all the fixings. In a corner stood a ten-foot spruce fully decorated. The piney scent mixed with vanilla and cinnamon filled the room with a relaxing feeling of warmth enhanced by the fire in the river-rock fireplace. A large maple mantel showcased rodeo trophies from every member of the Hart family.

He was home.

But he felt as if he'd been dropped into enemy territory and he was waiting for the first round of fire. This time, he knew, he would be hit. There was no way of escaping the inevitable.

Ace approached him, carrying a baby in a pink blanket. "I want you to meet Emma, the first Hart grandchild."

"You have a daughter?"

"Yep. Isn't she beautiful?"

Tuf looked at the perfect baby face with swirls of blond hair. "Yes, she is. Does she have a mother?"

Ace frowned at him in that familiar way Tuf remembered well, especially when Tuf had done something to displease him, like wearing Ace's best boots to a rodeo. "Of course—Flynn."

"McKinley?"

Ace's frown deepened to a point of aggravation until Flynn walked up. "Don't look so surprised, Tuf," the beautiful blonde said.

"How did you manage to lasso him?"

She leaned over and whispered, "It wasn't easy, but I finally found the magic rope." She winked and gently took her daughter from Ace. "She's only three weeks old and all this celebrating is too much for her. I'll put her in the bassinet in Sarah's room."

"Congratulations," Tuf said to his brother.

"Thanks. Glad you're home," Ace replied, but Tuf felt he wanted to say a whole lot more. They both knew this wasn't the time. Ace was the oldest, the responsible one and the head of the family, next to their mom. And Ace would hold Tuf accountable for two years of silence, two years of ignoring the family and two years of shirking his responsibility to said family. Accountability was coming but it would not be tonight.

His other brother, Colt, edged his way toward them. "Now, Ace kind of fibbed about the firstborn Hart grandchild." Colt pulled a boy of about eleven or twelve toward him. "This is Evan, my son."

Tuf stared at the boy and then back to his sandy-haired, handsome brother. Love-'em-and-leave-'em Colt—that's how he was known around the rodeo circuit. Romancing the ladies came easily to him, while Tuf found it almost painful sometimes. Maybe because his brothers cast long shadows and it was hard to walk in their wake. Seemed as if all his life he'd been trying to prove he was tough enough to match his older brothers and cousins.

"Nice to meet you," the boy said and held out his hand.

Tuf took it. "Nice to meet you, too, Evan." The last time Tuf was home, there had been no mention of Evan, and now wasn't the time to point that out.

Reaching behind him, Colt pulled a brown-haired woman forward. *Leah Stockton.* "You know Leah. We're married and these are her kids, five-year-old Jill and three-year-old Davey."

Tuf touched his forehead. "Am I in another time zone or something? Colt is married with a ready-made family?"

Colt punched Tuf's shoulder. "You bet."

Leah hugged him. "Welcome home, Tuf."

After that he was lost in a sea of unfamiliar faces. His cousin Duke strolled over with his new wife, Angie, and her eight-year-old son, Luke. He also met the new bride, Sierra, and his uncle Josh's wife, Jordan, who walked with a white cane and had a yellow Lab Seeing Eye dog named Molly. He didn't get the whole story, but he could see Uncle Josh was very much in love.

Seemed Sierra owned the Number 1 Diner in town and Jordan was her aunt. He was beginning to think there was something in the water. In the past year, his whole family had gotten married.

His mom shoved a plate of food into his hands. "Eat. We'll talk later."

He picked at the food, his eyes going to Dinah and Austin. That marriage still puzzled him. Buddy Wright was an alcoholic. Austin had said many times he would never be like his father, but Tuf had seen him at rodeos where he could barely stand. Tuf liked Austin, even though he had a problem holding his liquor. He didn't understand how he and Dinah had gotten together.

Finding a vacant chair, he sat down and continued to nibble at his food. Dinah slipped into the chair beside him.

"You know, you have a lot of explaining to do."

"Yeah." He speared a piece of prime rib. No one had enough guts to bring up the past two years tonight but his sister. She always danced to the sound of an offbeat drummer.

"But I'll give you time to settle in before I grill you."

"I'd appreciate that."

"You do know I'm the sheriff now, right?"

He glanced at her. "Mom mentioned it. If I see you in town with a gun on your hip, you'll have to forgive me if I laugh."

She frowned. "You better not."

"So you and Austin, huh?"

"Yeah. I love him and he's changed. He really has."

He stirred the meat into mashed potatoes. "A lot of that going around." Home was different now and he wondered how he'd fit in. They'd all moved on without him. He felt a little lonely in a room full of loving family.

"Mmm." Dinah kissed his cheek. "Welcome home, lil' brother."

Soon after, he said his good-nights and made his way to the stairs. His mom followed.

"Your room is ready. I washed the sheets every week just in case you'd come home."

Guilt the size of a boulder landed on his chest and he took a deep breath. The worry he must have caused her was too painful to think about.

His room was the same as he'd left it. Horseshoe patterns decorated the curtains and comforter. Horseshoes were branded into the headboard and the dresser—something he'd done when he was about twelve, much to his parents' disapproval. He had a thing about horses. All the

Hart kids did, but he was the only one who'd branded his furniture.

Chaps lay across a chair and he picked them up. "I don't think these will fit anymore."

"No, you've filled out."

On a bulletin board attached to the wall were newspaper clippings of some of his rodeo adventures in bareback riding. Belt buckles lay in a tray. His youth was in this room. He turned to see his mom staring at him.

"Go back to the party, Mom. I'm tired from the long drive and I'm just going to bed."

She lifted an eyebrow. "I would ask a long drive from where, but I know you'll tell me when you're ready."

"Mom…" That boulder got heavier on his chest.

She wrapped her arms around him and hugged. "I'm so happy you're home, my son."

He swallowed. "I'm home to stay."

"Good." She touched his face. "I'll see you in the morning."

As the door closed, he laid the chaps on the bed and walked over to the window. His room faced Thunder Road. Pushing the curtains aside, he glanced toward Buddy Wright's place and thought of Cheyenne. What was she doing back in Roundup? Was it for a visit? Or was she here to stay? He couldn't seem to get her out of his head, especially that tortured look in her eyes.

Almost ten years and he was right back where he'd started—dreaming of Cheyenne.

IN THE DAYS THAT FOLLOWED, everyone gave him his space, even Dinah, and he was grateful for that. He was used to getting up early and was usually out of the house by 5:00 a.m. Since it was still dark, he'd jog around the barns and inspect all the new additions. An updated mare motel had been built to house pregnant mares. Webcams monitored the activity of the mares. Ace had his vet practice set up in another barn with private stalls for his four-legged patients. The office for the ranch was next to that.

Cattle carriers, trailers and trucks were parked to the right of the barn. They sported a new logo: Hart Rodeo Contractors arched across the top, the lettering green. In the center was the Bull Mountains shadowed by a blue cloud with a bucking horse and bull in front. Below was etched Roundup, Montana. Very impressive. The family had invested heavily in the contracting business.

As soon as the sun peeked over the Bull Mountains, he saddled up Sundance, his brown quarter horse with a white blaze on his face, and galloped off into miles of Thunder Ranch. Snow blanketed the ground, but in places winter grass poked through. He stopped and sucked in the fresh, cold air. There was no scent anywhere like winter in Montana.

He kneed Sundance and rode along Thunder Creek. The snow-banked water was frozen in places. Sundance picked his way through the snow and Engelmann spruce, and they came across a herd of cattle huddled together near a windmill. At the sight of horse and rider, the cows bellowed. Tuf dismounted and saw the water trough had frozen over. Picking up a pipe left there for such purposes, he broke the ice. Cows milled around for a drink.

He swung into the saddle and was surprised not to see more cattle. The herd must have been downsized—more changes. He rode back to the house in time for breakfast.

When Tuf was in Afghanistan, he often dreamed of his mom's warm yellow kitchen with the pine plank floors, the natural butcher-block counters and cherry-stained cabinets. It relaxed him and he'd wondered if he'd ever sit at the family table again.

He ran his hand across the butcher-block table and felt the warmth of being home.

His mom watched him while he ate. She did that a lot, and he felt guilt press on his chest again.

Picking up his mug of coffee, he asked, "What happened to all the cattle?"

She shrugged. "The economy tanked and cattle prices dropped and I made the decision to downsize. The contracting business is time-consuming, and we need every available hand to make it a success."

He pushed back his plate. "Then I'll take care of the cattle. That should help."

"Yes, but I'd rather you enjoy life for a while. There's no rush for you to do anything."

That puzzled him. Growing up it was always important that everyone pulled their weight. "Come on, Mom. I need to stay busy. What is everyone else doing?"

"Ace handles the breeding program while Colt's in charge of Midnight and handles the rodeo bookings and transporting bucking horses. Beau and Josh take care of the bulls, though Josh is cutting back to spend more time with Jordan."

"Is anyone rodeoing?"

"You bet. There's a lot of rodeo talent in the Hart and Adams families. All the boys are riding to earn extra money for the ranch, except Duke. He's given up bull riding for Angie, but he's still helping to transport stock to rodeos."

He got up and poured another cup of coffee. "I never thought Duke would give up bull riding for love."

His mother carried dishes to the sink. "His heart was never in it like Beau's." She shot him a glance as she rinsed dishes to go in the dishwasher. "Like you."

"Yeah." He leaned against the counter. "I loved bareback riding."

"Your father said you're the best he'd ever seen."

He thought for a minute. "If everyone's rodeoing to make money, I can, too."

His mother had a way of not frowning, but she made up for that with a disapproving look.

"What?"

"For eight years I've gone to bed every night wondering if I'd ever see my youngest again."

"Mom..." His heart twisted.

"I just want you safe."

He smiled at her worried face. "We're the Harts. Rodeo is in our blood."

"Mmm. I guess it's safer than what you were doing."

"I want to help out." He tried to ease the tension.

"As long as I know someone's not pointing a gun at you, I..." She reached for a dish towel, wiped her hands and then dabbed at her eyes.

His heart twisted so tight he could barely breathe.

Ask me questions. Ask me. Let me get it off my chest.

But she didn't.

As she loaded the dishwasher, he had second thoughts. She was all alone in a five-bedroom house and that bothered him. His mom was used to having family around her. Ace had lived in the house with a separate entrance until his marriage. Now he lived at the McKinley place with his new family. Colt and Uncle Josh had houses nearby, but it wasn't the same thing.

There was a housekeeper, Lisa Marie, but she was only there a few hours a day to help his mother. He found that odd since his mom had always refused help. What had happened to change her mind?

She straightened and hugged him. A whiff of gardenia

reached him. It was a scented lotion she'd used ever since he could remember.

"Take all the time you need. When you're ready, you'll know. Now I have to get dressed and go to work. Lisa Marie will be here soon and Leah's probably already in the office."

"Leah takes care of the books now?"

"Yes, and she's been a blessing. All this new technology goes over my head sometimes. You'll have to check out the updated office. With the rodeo contracting busines we have to keep up-to-date records and know exactly where and when our animals go to rodeos. It takes all of us to accomplish that."

"Mmm. When are Uncle Josh and Beau coming back?" Seemed his uncle had gotten married a few weeks ago and they had gone on a honeymoon, too.

"Any day." His mom moved toward her bedroom.

"Mom, I need some new clothes. Is there anyplace in Roundup I can buy them?"

She glanced over her shoulder. "Austin carries nice things at his Western Wear and Tack Shop. It's not a law but a rule that you support family."

He grinned. "Yes, ma'am." He reached for his hat, slipped into his jacket and headed for the door. As he walked to his truck, he saw Midnight in a pen, and Gracie, one of the ranch hands, watching him. He strolled over to take a look. Gracie was somewhere in her forties and she knew her way around horses and cows. Bundled up in a heavy winter coat, she had a wool scarf looped over her felt hat and tied beneath her chin to cover her ears.

"Mornin', Tuf," she called and opened a large gate to a big corral. Midnight trotted through and galloped around kicking up his hooves in the nippy morning air.

"Mornin'." He leaned on the fence and watched. The

stallion circled the corral, his muscles rippling with restless energy.

"He's easy to exercise," Gracie said, "as long as I don't try to box him in. Though he loads pretty nicely into a trailer for Colt. You just have to know what to do and what not to do. The horse is temperamental, to say the least."

"But a gold mine if he performs as planned."

"You got it."

Midnight threw up his head, steam coming from his flared nostrils, but it was clear the horse reveled in the cold.

"He was born to buck," Tuf murmured.

"The family still hasn't decided yet." Gracie shoved her gloved hands into her jacket pockets. "It's cold. I hope Buddy gets here soon so I can go to the mare barn where it's warmer."

Tuf frowned. "Buddy Wright?"

"Yeah. When Midnight went missing, he showed up at Buddy's place with a few cuts. Buddy doctored his wounds and took care of him. He was afraid to tell anyone where the horse was because he feared everyone would think he'd stolen the Harts' prized stallion."

Tuf remembered Royce saying something about that.

"But Dinah got to the bottom of everything, and your mom was very grateful to Buddy. She encouraged him to visit Midnight at Thunder Ranch whenever he wanted. And he does about two or three times a week. It helps me out a lot."

Before Tuf could sort through this new information, Ace drove up to his clinic area and Colt pulled in behind him. They waved and went inside. They were giving him his space, and he should be happy about that, but in truth, he didn't understand it. If one of them or Beau or Duke had disappeared for two years without a word, he'd be mad as hell. But he was the one who'd left Thunder Ranch and his family. They had gotten used to life without him. Deep in his heart, though, he knew this standoff wasn't going to last. Soon someone would pop the cork of their bottled-up emotions and Tuf would be held accountable for his decisions.

ON HIS WAY INTO TOWN, he passed the Wright property. All was quiet, not a soul in sight. It was nice to know the Harts and Wrights were getting along so well. Very nice. He wondered if Cheyenne's husband was with her. Or if she had a husband. From the look in her eyes, he knew something bad had happened in her life. What?

He was thinking too much about her and turned his attention to the view. It hadn't snowed in days, but it still lingered across the landscape and nestled in the ponderosa pines. The chilly blue sky went on forever, and he was sure it reached into eternity with its wondrous breadth and depth. There weren't skies like that in Afghanistan.

As he turned onto Main Street, he looked for a parking spot near Austin's store. He swerved into a space and removed his keys. He'd purchased the silver Ford Lariat pickup in Maryland because he needed a way to get around. First new truck he'd ever owned, but he figured he'd earned it, since his pay had been piling up in his checking account. But he should have thought that over a little more. His mom said things were tight and the ranch could have used the money. Readjusting to the real world was a hell of a blow.

Getting out, he locked the doors, pocketed the keys and walked into Wright's Western Wear and Tack. A bell jangled over the door and the scent of leather reached him. He came to a complete stop.

Cheyenne was behind a counter, arranging colorful jewelry in a glass case. She looked up, her green eyes startled.

Her red hair was clipped behind her head and strands dangled around her pretty face. A flashback hit him that had nothing to do with Afghanistan. He was seventeen years old and sitting in the school auditorium right behind Cheyenne Wright, staring at the back of her hair pinned up much like it was today. Several loose strands curled against the curve of her neck, and he'd wondered if he reached out with one finger and gently tugged her hair toward his lips if it would taste like cinnamon. Which was odd, because Cheyenne never gave him any indication she wanted him to taste any part of her.

Strange how that memory lingered in his mind.

"Can I help you?" she asked in the coolest voice he'd ever heard.

Chapter Three

Cheyenne's heart pounded in her chest at an alarming rate—too alarming to suit her. What was Tuf doing here? And why was he still standing at the door?

Closing the glass case with a snap, she asked again, "Can I help you with something?"

He removed his hat like a true gentleman and stepped closer to her. Well over six feet with wide shoulders, he was a little intimidating, which she was made very aware of by the flutter in her stomach. His dark brown hair was cut short and neat, and the lines of his face were all sharp bones and angles. A tiny scar over his left cheek added to his manly image.

The scar wasn't something new. He'd had it in school. Rumor was he'd fallen off a horse when he was about three and hit a water trough.

"Is Austin here?"

She cleared her throat. "No…no, he's over at the diner having coffee with Dinah. He should be back shortly."

"Oh." He looked around. "I need some clothes. Do you mind if I look around?"

"Um…no." Was she supposed to help him? Why couldn't he wait until Austin returned?

He settled his hat onto his head and glanced at the items

on racks and shelves. Without taking time to look at anything, he grabbed T-shirts, socks, long johns and Jockey shorts.

He wears briefs.

Cheyenne took a deep breath. She really didn't need to know that.

After laying his load on the counter, he walked to a round rack of Western shirts. He found his size and reached for a handful. Good heavens, he didn't even look at the style or the color. Unable to stand it, she made her way to his side and tried not to frown.

"Don't you want to look at the shirts?"

"No. Why?"

She suppressed a groan. "They're different. Some are solids, prints, plaids and checks."

"Doesn't matter. It's a shirt."

She gritted her teeth. "Some have snaps. Some have buttons."

"Doesn't matter. I can handle both."

"This is ridiculous. No one buys clothes without looking at them."

He shrugged. "I've been buying my clothes since I was about sixteen and that's my method."

That would account for that god-awful shirt he wore in school.

He pointed to her face. "You're frowning. What's wrong with the way I buy clothes?"

Now she'd stepped in it. Why was she even talking to him? She should have stayed at the counter. She bit her lip and stepped in a little deeper. "I was remembering that bright pumpkin-orange shirt with purple piping you wore in school. Evidently you had on sunglasses when you bought it."

He gave a cocky grin. "Ah, the orange shirt. My friends

and I were in Billings getting rodeo supplies and they had that shirt in the window. I said someone would have to pay me to wear something so gaudy. Well, that's what my friends did. They bought it and paid me twenty bucks to wear it to school. It got a lot of attention and laughs. I'm sure I still have it. My mom never throws anything away. It's too small for me now, but you can have it if you like." He lifted a daring eyebrow.

"No, thanks." She took the shirts out of his hands and held one up. "This is a solid baby-blue Western with pearl snaps. It comes in white, yellow and pink. You might prefer the yellow."

His grin widened and she felt a kick to her lower abdomen. "No. I prefer the blue."

"See. That's shopping. Making a decision." She held up another. "This is a light blue check. We have it in dark blue, too."

"I'll take the dark blue."

"And this—" she pulled a shirt off the rack "—is red, white and blue. It was made popular by Garth Brooks. Since you're a former marine, you might like it."

"I do." He glanced at the shirt and then at her. "But don't you think it's a little loud?"

It was, but she wasn't going to admit that after the orange-shirt comment. "It's fine."

"Good. I'll take three."

She had a feeling he didn't really care. To him it was just a shirt, like he'd said. She found that so strange. Her husband, Ryan, had been a picky dresser. Sometimes she took shirts back three or four times before she could find one he liked. And they had to be starched and ironed before he'd wear them. If they weren't... Her hand instinctively went to her cheek.

"Do you have any chambray shirts and jeans?" He glanced at the shirts hung against a wall.

"Yes." She waved her hand. "And Austin has a lot more on this round rack. What color?"

"Light blue."

"Not red?"

"No. That's Colt's trademark. Too flashy."

"Yeah, right." She reached for two. "Jeans are here." She pointed to her left. "The size is beneath each stack. Do you know your size?"

He stared directly at her with steamy dark eyes. "Doesn't every man?"

She felt dizzy, but she just shrugged. "You'd be surprised. A lot of women buy their husband's clothes."

"I don't have a wife, and like I told you, I buy my own clothes." He studied the sizes and fit and pulled out five pairs.

"Mommy, Sadie's coloring on my page."

"Excuse me." She took the shirts and jeans from him, and as hard as she tried not to touch him, his hand brushed against hers in a fleeting reminder of the difference in the texture of male skin. She drew in a breath, laid the merchandise on the counter and went to her daughters, who sat at a small table in a corner.

"Sadie, color in your own book." She homeschooled the girls, and while she worked in the store, they did their lessons. Today they were coloring a picture according to the colors Cheyenne had marked on the page.

"Sammie doesn't know how to color. I'm just showing..." Sadie's green eyes widened and her mouth fell open. Cheyenne knew why. Tuf was standing behind her. She could feel his warm vibes.

She stepped aside. "I don't believe you've formally met my daughters. Girls, this is Tuf Hart, Aunt Dinah's brother.

And this is Cassandra and Samantha. Otherwise known as Sadie and Sammie."

"Why not call her Sandy or Cassie?"

Cheyenne tensed. "It's a name her father gave her."

Tuf nodded and looked at the girls. "Nice to meet you."

Sadie scrunched up her face. "I don't like you."

"That seems to be a unanimous opinion in the Wright family."

Cheyenne forced herself not to smile. "Sadie, that's not nice. Apologize."

Her spirited daughter hung her head.

"Sadie."

Sadie mumbled something, and Cheyenne went to the checkout counter with Tuf. "My name is Sundell now," she said and was unsure of the reason why she needed to mention that.

"So you and your husband moved back to Roundup?"

Cheyenne kept scanning the items into the cash register, trying not to react. Trying to be cool. "No. Just the girls and me."

There was a pregnant pause filled with all kinds of questions. But again, she didn't react. "Will there be anything else?"

"I need PRCA regulated rowels and spurs."

"Austin orders those."

"I figured." He reached for his wallet in his back pocket and pulled out a credit card.

She totaled his purchases, swiped his card and ripped off a receipt for him to sign. She watched as his strong hand slashed out *Tomas Hart.* No one around here called him that. Even in school he was always known as Tuf, the youngest Hart.

As he slipped the card back into his wallet, he said, "I

was out of line the other day. Your child is your business and I shouldn't have said a word."

She was taken aback by the apology, but all of Sarah Hart's children had good manners. "No, you shouldn't have, but I appreciate your concern. Sadie always tests my patience."

He nodded and picked up the big bag from the counter as if it weighed no more than his wallet. "Thanks for the help."

Even though she told herself not to, she watched through the display window as he took long strides back to his silver truck.

"Mommy, who's that man?"

Cheyenne looked down to see Sadie staring up at her with big green eyes.

Someone I knew a long time ago. Someone I wished I'd had the courage to date.

"He's Aunt Dinah's brother."

Sadie bobbed her head. "Aunt Dinah gots lots of brothers."

Sammie leaned into her, wrapping herself as close as she could to Cheyenne, needing attention, love and reassurance that their world was still okay. Sometimes she didn't know if she had that much strength because she struggled every day to make sense of a life blown apart. But for her daughters she would do everything possible to hide her fears.

Her eyes strayed to the window. If only she could go back in time…

TUF GLANCED ACROSS THE STREET at the redbrick building that used to be the home of the old newspaper but was now the Number 1 Diner. Sierra, Beau's wife, owned it, and Tuf's mother raved about the home cooking. He swung the bag of clothes into the backseat of his truck and walked over.

Inside, the diner was decorated in a mining theme, and he remembered his mom saying it had been named in honor of Sierra's grandfather, who'd died in a mine. On the walls were mining photos and a long shelf held mining artifacts. The tables were red and the chairs had black leather seats. The place had a rustic, homey appeal, and the scent coming from the kitchen made him hungry.

He spotted Dinah and Austin sitting close together in a booth. Not wanting to interrupt, he started for the counter to order coffee, but Austin eased out of the booth, so Tuf strolled over to join them.

"Hey, Tuf." Austin shook his hand.

"I was just over at your shop to order some rowels, spurs and chaps."

Austin's eyebrows rose. "Getting back into rodeoing?"

"Yeah."

"Come back and I'll get you set up."

"Okay. I'll visit with my sister first."

"Good deal." Austin leaned down to kiss Dinah and then made his way toward the door. Dinah's eyes followed him and she had a dreamy look on her face.

Tuf slid into the booth. "You've got it bad, Sheriff."

Her gaze swung to him. "Yes, I do."

Tuf removed his hat and placed it beside him. Before he could say anything, a young girl in jeans with a red apron trimmed in black appeared to take his order.

"Just coffee, please."

When the girl left, Dinah asked, "So you're getting back into rodeoing?"

"Mom and I talked about it. She'd rather I take it easy for a while, but I need to be busy."

"Maybe you've been taking it easy for two years. Who knows?"

This was the Dinah he knew, the one who came straight to the point, spoke her mind and didn't pussyfoot around.

"But I'm not going to grill you because I know you've been through a great deal."

Damn. She was folding like a greenhorn in Vegas. He didn't expect that. He should just tell her where he'd been, and he didn't understand what was holding him back.

The waitress placed a cup of hot coffee in front of him, and his hand gripped the warmth of the cup. But words lodged in his throat.

"Are you okay?" Dinah asked in a concerned voice. "That's all I want to know."

"I'm fine." He took a sip of coffee and thought it best to change the subject. "I saw Cheyenne over at the store."

"She helps out when Austin needs her. Aren't her little girls adorable?" Dinah looked down and rubbed the swell of her stomach. "I hope our little one is as cute."

"How could it not? His or her mother is a natural beauty."

"Stop it." Dinah wrinkled her nose. "You're my brother. You have to say that."

He grinned. "Not really. That's Austin's job. Me, I can poke fun all I want. It comes by right of birth." He pointed to her chest. "Love the way that badge sparkles on your khaki shirt there." He leaned over to see her waist. "Damn. No gun."

"Will you stop?" Her voice was stern, but her eyes sparkled.

He took a sip of coffee, remembering all the times he'd teased her as a kid. It was part of his job as little brother. Her teen years were a nightmare. John Hart kept a tight rein on his only daughter, and Dinah rebelled over and over. Tuf often wondered if Dinah would make it through those turbulent times. He would tease her just to see her smile.

Dinah scooted to the end of the booth. "I have to get back to work."

"What's Cheyenne's situation?" he asked before he could stop himself.

She sighed. "Please tell me you've gotten over that teenage crush."

"I have." He twisted his cup. "I'm just curious. She's different."

"She's going through a rough time."

"She said her husband wasn't with her in Roundup."

"No." Dinah dug in her purse and laid some bills on the table.

"Are they divorced?"

She frowned at him. "No. He died."

"Oh." He wasn't expecting that. "Cancer, heart..."

"Tuf." His sister actually glared at him. "Cheyenne's emotions are very fragile right now and..."

"What happened to her husband?"

Her glare was now burning holes through him. "You can't let this go, can you?"

"Like I told you, I'm curious. There's a certain sadness about her, and I know something traumatic has happened in her life."

Dinah zipped her purse. "Okay. But what I tell you, you keep to yourself. Very few people in Roundup know this, and I don't want people gossiping behind her back."

"Have you ever known me to gossip?"

"No, and that's why I'm telling you." She drew a deep breath. "Her husband was a marine."

"He died in combat?"

"No. He was out for six months and had severe PTSD.

Austin said he had terrible nightmares and was sometimes violent."

A knot formed in his stomach and bile rose in his throat. He fought the terrible memories every day, and he vowed they would not bring him down. He'd stand strong. He was a marine. But there were days…

"What happened?"

"He left a note for Cheyenne saying he was leaving and not to try and find him. He added they were better off without him. Two days later he was found in a motel. He'd shot himself."

"Oh, God." Now he knew what the look in Cheyenne's eyes was about. The life she'd planned was not the life she was living. She'd learned that there was hatred and evil in the world and it had spread to the most innocent victims like herself and her daughters. Her belief in life had been shattered, and she was struggling to make sense of it all—like he was.

"I'm sorry she had to go through that," he murmured.

"We all are." Dinah reached across the table and rubbed his forearm. "Are you sure you're okay?"

"Yep." He reached for his hat. "I'll walk you to your office."

Dinah got to her feet. "Oh, please. I'm the sheriff, remember?"

Tuf stood with a smile. But he still had an ache inside for all the soldiers who had come home and were still fighting that terrible war in their minds.

"Look," Dinah said, and he followed her gaze to the kitchen area. Beau stood there. He kissed Sierra and headed for the front door.

"Hey, Beau," Tuf called.

Beau swung around and walked toward them with a grin on his face.

"You're home," Tuf said.

"We got back late last night. I spoke with Dad, and he and Jordan just drove in, too. I'm picking up Duke at the sheriff's office, and we're going out to welcome them home."

"Sounds like a plan." Dinah stepped toward the door. "I'll go with you to the office to make sure we don't have anything pressing. See you at the ranch." She waved to Tuf.

Tuf made his way across the street to his truck. As he was about to get in, he noticed Sadie and Sammie looking through the glass door of the shop. He raised a hand in greeting. Surprisingly, they both lifted a hand, but they didn't smile. He knew without a doubt they were affected by their father's death. Cheyenne shooed them back to their seats, and their eyes locked for a moment. So much sadness clouded her beautiful face. He got in his truck and drove away, telling himself it was none of his business.

And he was real good at lying to himself.

WHEN HE REACHED THE RANCH, he saw Ace's and Colt's trucks parked near Ace's vet office. He drove there, too. As he got out, he heard loud voices coming from the barn attached to the office.

"It's time, Ace," Colt was saying. "Midnight has healed and we need to get him on the rodeo circuit as soon as February."

"No way. I'm not risking him getting hurt again. Breeding season is about to start and he'll be busy."

"Damn it. Can't you see how restless he is? He needs the excitement of the rodeo."

"I agree," Tuf said before he thought it through.

His brothers swung around to stare at him. It wasn't a good stare. His settling-in period was over.

Ace's eyes narrowed on him. "You haven't shown any

interest in this ranch for eight years and now you think you have a say?"

"Yeah, Tuf," Colt added. "We understand about the first six years. You were fighting a war, but where in the hell have you been for the last two?"

Ace had a lot more to say. "Do you even realize how bad it's been around here? We had to lease a lot of our land and take out a mortgage with my vet business on the line to survive. Everyone pulled their weight to make sure Thunder Ranch didn't go under."

"I didn't know."

"No, because you never called home to find out." Cool, collected Ace had reached a breaking point, and Tuf knew he had every right to be upset. "You never even called home to check on Mom. That I can't forgive. Do you know she had a spell with her heart and was hospitalized for a few days? We had no way to get in touch with you."

He felt as if he'd been kicked in the gut by the wildest bronc in Montana. He swallowed. "Mom had my cell number. I gave it to her when I called that one time."

"No." Ace shook his head. "Mom would have told me."

"I had it," their mom said from the doorway. Uncle Josh, Beau, Duke and Dinah stood behind her.

"What?" The color drained from Ace's face. "But you asked me to call his friends to see if Tuf had contacted them."

The group walked farther into the barn until they stood in a circle. Horses neighed, and Royce and Gracie came in through a side door. But everyone was staring at his mom.

"Yes, I did," Sarah admitted. "I was worried and wanted to know if Tomas had reached out to some of his old buddies. They would talk to you quicker than an overprotective mother. I'm sorry, Ace. I know I lean on you too much."

"It's okay, Mom," Ace assured her. "It's not your fault. It's Tuf's."

Tuf took the blow to his heart like a marine, like a cowboy, without flinching. It was his fault, and it was time to open that wound and let it bleed until he couldn't feel the pain anymore.

Uncle Josh patted his shoulder, and Tuf hadn't even realized he'd moved toward him. "We don't mean to pressure you, Tuf, but you're a part of this family and we've all been worried. It's not like you to shut the family out. If you found someone and wanted to spend some time with her, we'd all understand. We just need to know why you've ignored us for two years."

"There isn't anyone," he murmured under his breath.

"Were you injured and in a hospital?" Dinah asked.

"No. It wasn't that."

He looked at their expectant faces and knew he had to tell them. They deserved the truth. But once he did, they would look at him differently.

And he didn't know if he was ready to handle different.

Chapter Four

Tuf couldn't put it off any longer.

Accountability had arrived.

He held up his hands and took two steps backward. "Okay. Just listen. Don't say anything until I'm through."

Everyone nodded, except his mom.

"This is ridiculous," she said. "You don't have to tell us a thing if you don't want to."

Ace flung a hand toward Tuf. "Stop protecting him. You always do that. Tuf's old enough and strong enough to take responsibility for his own actions."

"Why did you start this?" his mom demanded of Ace. "I told you to leave it alone."

Ace sighed and turned away.

His mother instinctively knew he'd been through something horrific, and she was doing everything she could to protect him. Shielding her kids from pain had been her life's work, but Tuf couldn't take the easy way out. Not this time.

"Ace is right," he told his mother. "I have to take responsibility for the last two years, so please just listen." He stared down at the dirt floor. "I was all set to come home. My commander said the paperwork was in order. One more mission and I was going to be flown to Germany for evaluation and then to a base in the U.S. and finally home. I couldn't wait to get back to Thunder Ranch and family."

He took a deep breath and stared at the corner post of a horse stall. "The insurgents had attacked a small village that they suspected of giving aid to U.S. Marines. Most of them were able to get out but two families were trapped. Our orders were to go in a back way in the dead of night and rescue the Afghans. An Afghan soldier guided us through rocky terrain to the village. Getting in undetected was no problem. We found four adults and three kids in a mud-walled hut. Dawn was about to break and we had to get them out quickly. Then we were informed by the Afghan soldier that there was an elderly woman trapped in another hut. We found her and brought her to the others.

"When we were finally ready to leave, daylight broke. For some reason a little girl about three darted for the doorway. PFC Michael Dobbins was closest to her and he jumped to grab her. But it was too late. The insurgents knew we were there. They fired at Michael and he went down and fell on the girl. We immediately returned fire, but Michael was taking the brunt of the hits. His body jerked every time a bullet struck him. I told the corporal to call the commander and let him know what was happening and to call for mortar fire. We needed help."

His lungs expanded and his hands curled into fists as red flashes of gunfire blurred his eyes. "Then I charged out that door, firing blindly, and covered Michael's bloody body."

"No," Sarah cried, and Josh put his arm around her.

Tuf didn't pause or look at his mother. He couldn't. He had to keep talking.

"The rest of my unit joined me, and we made a wall in front of Michael to keep more bullets from hitting him. We just kept returning fire, and we all knew we were in the open and could very well die there. Then the order came, charge up that hill and take out the insurgents, so we hauled ass. A marine was hit and then the Afghan soldier went down. We found shelter behind some rocks and then we waited, hoping and praying that the attack chopper would come in soon with mortar fire."

He paused. "As soon as the blasts started, we continued our surge to the top. When we got there, six heavily armed insurgents came out of a cave. They fired on us, but we had the upper hand. It was over in seconds. We ran down that hill, picked up our two wounded men and headed for the rescue chopper. Everyone was shouting, 'Run, run, run,' but I kept thinking about Michael back at that hut. I couldn't leave him in that hellhole."

He unclenched his numb hands. "I ran in the other direction, and I could hear my men shouting for me to come back. We didn't know if more insurgents were in the area, and we were ordered to get out fast. But I still kept running toward that hut. I fell down by Michael. The mother and father of the little girl were there desperately trying to lift Michael's body off their child. He was a big man and deadweight. I helped them and the girl was still alive. On the ground was some sort of Muslim toy. The girl must have dropped it when they'd rushed into the hut to escape the insurgents. I handed it to her and realized the toy was the reason she'd run for the door. I pointed in the direction where the chopper was landing and told them to go. Then I hoisted Michael's blood-soaked body over my shoulder and followed.

"Everyone had already boarded, but the chopper waited for me. Two marines helped to carry Michael inside. I watched as a medic covered Michael's body with a blanket. He was dead. He was finally going home, too."

"Oh, no," his mother cried.

Tuf kept talking because he knew if he stopped he wouldn't be able to start again. "I leaned my head against the chopper wall, closed my eyes and imagined I was back at Thunder Ranch in Mom's kitchen eating peanut butter from a jar with my finger. I could see that look on Mom's face when I did things like that and I relaxed, wishing and praying I was away from that awful war. Away from the killing.

"I don't remember much about the next few days, but I was flown to Germany for evaluation and then to the San Diego base. I was going home and putting it behind me was all I could think about, but first I planned to go to the commander's office and ask for Michael's parents' address. I wanted to go see them and tell them what a hero their son was in saving the little girl's life. Before I could do that, I got a message my presence was requested in the commander's office. I thought he wanted to wish me well or something. I was unprepared for what he really wanted. He said to call my folks and let them know I wasn't coming home just yet. A plane was waiting to take me to the naval hospital in Bethesda, Maryland. Michael Dobbins was asking to see me."

A collective "oh" echoed around the dusty barn, and Tuf noticed Royce and Grace had taken seats on bales of alfalfa, listening intently.

"I was stunned but glad he was alive. I figured he wanted to thank me for carrying him out of there. I was mistaken. The doctor advised me to be prepared for the worst. But nothing could have prepared me for the sight of Michael. He was bandaged from head to toe. Tubes seemed to be attached to every part of his body. The gunfire had blown off the left side of his face. They'd amputated his left leg and he was in danger of losing his left arm. But Michael was refusing any more surgeries. He wanted to die."

He gulped a breath. "I stood there staring at his one good eye. The right side of his face and mouth were the only parts of him that weren't bandaged. A suffocating feeling came over me, and I didn't know what to say or what to do. Michael had plenty to say, though. 'Why couldn't you have left me there? Why did you have to play the hero and come back for me?' His strained voice demanded an answer. Again, I didn't know what to say. 'I hate you,' he screamed at me. 'I'd rather be dead. I have no life like this. Why did you have to save me?'

"I couldn't answer so I walked out. The doctor informed me that Michael was refusing to see his parents, his wife and their three-month-old son. I was the only one he'd asked to see. The doctor added that I was Michael's only hope. I was overwhelmed by the responsibility, and I wanted to leave that hospital and never look back. But I found I couldn't. All the years of Mom and Dad preaching morals, values and honor must have reached me. I went back into that room prepared for battle.

"As soon as I entered, Michael screamed, 'Get out.' I told him no. He'd asked for me and I wasn't leaving. He looked at the ceiling and refused to speak. I searched my brain for something to say, something to get his attention. I just started talking off the top of my head, telling him the cowboys around the rodeo circuit have a saying—when things get rough, 'cowboy up.' I reminded him it was time to 'marine up,' to fight for the most precious thing he had—his life. He kept staring at the ceiling, and I kept talking, saying stuff like cowboys and marines don't give up and if he did, he wasn't the man I thought he was."

Tuf felt as though he was back in that hospital room. He could smell the antiseptic, hear the beep of the heart monitor. He swallowed hard.

"Out of the blue Michael asked if cowboys died with

their boots on. 'Hell, yes,' I said, 'and it's even better to die in the arms of a beautiful woman.' He seemed to relax and I could swear he was smiling. I felt I was getting through to him so I kept pressuring him, telling him how much he needed the surgeries. Finally, I asked in a loud voice, 'Marine, what's your answer?'

"He didn't say anything for a long time and then he asked if I would stay with him. That threw me. I reminded him that his wife and parents were waiting. He said he didn't want them to see him like he was. I heard the pain in his voice and I found myself agreeing to stay. I told the doctor the surgeries were a go and then I called Mom to tell her I couldn't come home, but I would as soon as I could. I gave her my cell number in case she needed to get in touch with me."

Nobody said a word and Tuf forced himself to finish the story. "After the first surgery, I figured I'd leave, but it took six surgeries to repair his arm. Janet, Michael's wife, haunted the lobby, but Michael refused to see her. I felt sorry for her and I didn't know how to get through to Michael. I slept on a bed in his room, and every night I pushed him about seeing his wife. He finally admitted his fears about his face. A part of his jaw and cheekbone were missing as was his eye. He was going to look different and he wasn't sure his wife could take that. In a way I understood his fears, and I stayed as the doctors started reconstructive surgery to his face. Days turned into weeks, weeks into months. Thanksgiving and Christmas came, and I sat through every painstaking surgery praying and hoping that Michael was going to find the strength to live again."

He drew in deeply. "After calling Mom, I'm sorry I never called home again. I felt guilty and conflicted about Michael. I kept wondering if I'd done him any favors by saving his life. I kept thinking it was my fault he was going through so much pain. If I hadn't played the hero, like he'd said, he wouldn't be suffering, but I could never make myself believe that. All I knew was I had to stay there to help him heal. I had to really save him this time. If I had spoken to anyone here and heard of Mom's health scare or the ranch's financial situation, I wouldn't have been able to do that because I wanted to come home so badly."

"Oh, my poor sweet son." His mother rushed to him and wrapped her arms around him. He clung to her because his legs felt weak. "Don't you apologize for a thing."

"Did Michael recover?" Ace asked in a low voice.

"Yes. It was difficult, but the reconstructive surgeries to his face were amazing. They rebuilt his cheekbone and jawbone, and he received a new artificial hand-painted eye. It looked real. There were scars, but they were hardly noticeable. This was when I told Michael it was time to see his wife. He didn't know it, but I'd been sending her pictures of Michael from my phone when he wasn't looking. She needed to see that he was alive and healing. I told him if he didn't see her, I was leaving. He sat in a chair stone-faced and I headed for the door."

His mom patted his chest. "He saw her?"

"Not until I forced him," he replied. "Before I could reach the door, he reminded me I'd told him that cowboys live by a code of honor and they always keep their word. He added I wasn't a true cowboy if I left. He had me and it made me mad. I pulled out my phone and informed him that this is how a cowboy would handle the situation. I sent a text to Janet to come to the room. Now Michael was angry, but I told him not to worry. I had his back.

"It was a Saturday, and Michael's parents had brought his son to visit Janet. When she entered the room, she held the boy by the hand. He was over a year old now and walking. He tottered over to Michael, who was sitting in a chair, and said 'Da-da.' A tear slipped from Michael's right eye and I quietly left the room. The counselor wanted to see me so I went to his office. He said it was time to wean Michael away from me. I was all for that. I never slept in Michael's room again. Janet finally moved in and I slept down the hall.

"The counselor advised me to do something I enjoyed away from the hospital. For me that's rodeoing, but I didn't have a way to get around so I bought a truck, got my rodeo card and signed up to ride. When Michael's parents came to see him, I thought I'd go home for a visit. I got as far as Wyoming, and I saw Beau at a rodeo and knew once I reached Thunder Ranch, I'd never be able to leave. I'd given Michael my word, so I headed back to Maryland. I'm sorry, Beau. I couldn't talk about it at the time."

"Don't worry," Beau said. "I was just concerned. You weren't yourself."

"He's home now." His mom patted his chest again. "That's what matters."

"As soon as Michael walked out of that hospital on his prosthetic leg with his wife and parents by his side, I headed for Montana." He reached into his pocket. "My unit was awarded the Bronze Star for bravery in protecting Michael. And Michael received the Silver Star for bravery in saving the little girl." He opened his hand to reveal a Silver Star encased in a clear plastic sheath. "I was awarded the Silver Star as well for covering Michael's body and for carrying him out of there." He held it out to his mother. "I want you to have it."

"No, no." She shook her head. "You keep it. You earned it, my son. You're the hero."

Suddenly, there was that silence he dreaded. He glanced at their familiar faces and saw the look he dreaded, too—

hero worship. He shoved the medal into his pocket and took a step backward. “I’m not a hero. Michael is. I did what I was trained to do. Anyone here would have done the same thing. Any marine in my unit would have done the same thing.”

Uncle Josh put his arm around Tuf’s shoulders. “But no one in your unit covered Michael’s body. No one in your unit ran back for him. They were running for the chopper and safety. You did that. Why is *hero* so hard for you to accept?”

“Because you’re looking at me different. I’m not different. I’m still the annoying younger brother.”

Ace approached him on the left side. “Yep, you’re still that annoying kid who had the nerve to wear my best boots to a rodeo, like I wouldn’t see the mud and the scuffs. But you’ll forgive me if I see a man where a boy used to stand.”

“Yeah.” Colt moved closer.

Dinah, Beau and Duke echoed the sentiment.

Some of the tension left him. “I know none of you understood my reasons for joining the marines, but when Dad died, I lost my love of rodeo. It wasn’t the same without him there. I was always in the shadows of my brothers and cousins. I had to get away to find my own niche in life. I just never planned on being away so long.” He sucked air into his starved lungs. He never talked this much. Ever. “I’m home now and I’m ready to start rodeoing again to help out.” He looked at Ace. “Just how bad are the finances?”

After a round of hugs and shaking hands, he, Ace and their mom walked to the office. For the next two hours, they went over the books with Leah. They’d leased three thousand acres to a man from Texas who was always late with the lease money. That put a strain on making the payment on a three-hundred-thousand-dollar note at the bank.

Seemed the economy, a flood and bad decisions made by their father had left the ranch deep in debt.

Tuf rose from his chair. "I'll go to the house and get my checkbook. I have some money in my account, and I'll sign it over to the ranch."

"Absolutely not," his mom said.

"Sorry, Mom, it's my money and I can do what I want with it and I can sell my truck."

"Slow down," Ace advised. "You're going to need a dependable truck if you start rodeoing."

"Yeah. I hadn't thought of that."

Ace patted his back. "I'm sorry I was short with you earlier."

"Come on, Ace, don't do that. Don't treat me with kid gloves. You've never done that before."

Ace nodded. "Okay, then get your ass to rodeoing and see how much money you can win."

"That I can do."

"But I want you to know I'm proud of what you did for Michael. Dad would be, too."

"Thank you." Emotions clogged his throat for a second, and he wondered why it had been so hard to open up and share his experience with his family. In the end it had been cathartic.

His family might look at him differently, but he knew they would never treat him differently.

That he could handle.

Chapter Five

Most of January Tuf busied himself learning the rodeo contracting business. Leah had a huge whiteboard in the office listing rodeos and horses and bulls to be delivered to said rodeos. He didn't see Midnight's name on the board. His mom hadn't made her decision yet.

"Tuf Hart, get away from my board," Leah said, walking into the office.

"Yes, ma'am." He grinned. If anyone got too close to that board, Leah was on the alert. She didn't want anyone messing with it. She was organized and thorough.

Since Uncle Josh wanted to spend more time with his wife, Tuf took over a lot of his chores, like taking care of the cows, but Ace planned to hire another hand when Tuf hit the rodeo circuit. Colt and Beau came in, and the three of them sat at the computer picking rodeos they were going to participate in and coordinating many events with the delivery of Hart animals to the rodeo.

"I'll participate some," Colt said, "but I got a kid and two stepkids, not to mention a wife I'm not getting far from."

"Thank you, honey," Leah said from her desk, not even raising her head.

Beau leaned back in his chair. "Sierra and I talked, and I'm going to give it my all this one last year."

Tuf knew Beau was worried about not being home for Sierra. She had a genetic eye disorder and would eventually go blind, but she was very independent and intended to stay that way.

"You and me, huh?" Tuf asked.

Beau thought for a moment. "Sierra's my top priority, but I'll stick with you as long as I can."

"What's your goal, Tuf?" Colt asked.

The answer was easy. "To make as much money as I can."

"How about the nationals in Vegas?" Colt pressed.

Tuf shrugged. "I'm a little rusty. We'll see how the year goes." Tuf leaned forward. "Can we use your Airstream trailer if we need it?"

"Sure."

"We're set, then." He slapped Beau on the back. "I run at five in the morning. Want to join me?"

Beau frowned. "Are you crazy? At five in the morning, I'll be wrapped around my wife."

"Wimp." Tuf laughed as he left the office.

AT FIVE THE NEXT MORNING, he got up and did his squats and stretches and then dressed in heavy sweats, sneakers, gloves and a wool cap. The temperature was in the thirties, but it wasn't snowing. To combat the darkness, he had reflectors on his jacket and sneakers. He planned to stay physically fit to compete. The cool morning air burned his lungs. Yet there was something uplifting about running when the world was asleep. An occasional truck sound and a coyote yapping accompanied him.

When he reached Roundup, the sun burst through the clouds, bathing the town in a misty yellow glow. He stopped at the sheriff's office to take a breather and had a cup of coffee with Duke, who had night duty.

"I—I don't know what to say to you," Duke mumbled, sitting at his desk. "I'm blown away by what you did in the Marine Corps."

"Seems like it happened to another person." It was always easy to talk to his quiet cousin. "I'm glad to put it behind me."

"Do you think about it much?"

"I try not to." He took a swig of the bitter coffee. He thought about it all the time, but no one needed to know that. And his greatest fear was sleep. That's when the nightmares came.

"If you need to talk, I work a lot of nights."

"How does Angie feel about that?"

"She's the best."

"Mmm." Tuf took another swig and got to his feet. "Thanks." He raised a hand in farewell. "See you later."

He ran toward Thunder Road and thought how nice it was that Duke had found the perfect partner, his soul mate. Ace, Colt, Beau and Dinah had also found their other half. He wasn't sure that was ever going to happen for him. It would have to be someone special—someone who was willing to share his nightmares.

The wind picked up, but he pressed on, monitoring his breathing, reserving his strength, something he'd learned in the marines. Suddenly he came to a complete stop. Up ahead, Sadie, wrapped up in her purple coat, was walking on the side of the road, head down, and trudging straight for him. Cheyenne was nowhere in sight.

About four feet from him, Sadie jumped back as she realized someone was standing in front of her.

He squatted. "Hey, munchkin, where you going?"

She shrugged.

"Where's your mother?"

She shrugged again.

"Let's go find her." He stood.

Sadie looked up at him. "Are you a stranger?"

"No. I've known your mother since we were kids."

"Oh."

He reached for her hand and she didn't object. Slowly they made their way to the Wright entrance and driveway. Cheyenne ran to meet them, Sammie trailing behind her.

"Sadie, where have you been?" she asked.

Sadie shrugged.

"I'm getting really upset by this behavior, Sadie. I…"

"I gotta pee, Mommy." Sammie clutched her crotch. "I gotta pee."

"Run to the house," Cheyenne told her.

"No. I'm scared." Sammie started to cry.

Turmoil etched Cheyenne's face as she struggled with her emotions, her attention split between her daughters.

"I'll watch Sadie," he offered.

"Thanks. We'll only be a minute." She grabbed Sammie's hand and they ran for the house.

Tuf still held Sadie's hand, and he lead her to the steps on the front porch. He sat on the top one and she perched beside him. It was evident that something was bothering Sadie. He didn't have to be a psychologist to know that. Going on a hunch, he tried to draw her out.

"When I was six, I ran away from home."

"You did?" Today Sadie had the hood over her head and the white fur lining circled her face. She looked like an angel.

"Yep."

"Why?"

"Well, I have two older brothers, an older sister and two older cousins. I was the youngest and I wasn't allowed to do what they did. I was too small. I wanted to be big and tough like them. When my dad wouldn't let me round up cows with them, I decided to leave and find a family without older, bigger kids."

The little girl watched him intently. "Where did you go?"

"I didn't get too far. My dad drove up and asked if I needed a lift into town. I got in the truck and he drove to Roundup. He asked if I wanted an ice cream at McDonald's. I said yes, and after that he said he was going to the feed store and I went along. A man with a horse in a trailer drove in behind us."

"Was it a pretty horse?"

"Oh, yes. A chestnut mare and she had a white star on her face. The man said his son went off to college and the horse was for sale. I told my dad we needed to buy it. He said he'd buy the horse if I'd take care of her. I agreed and named her Star. On the way home, Dad told me I wasn't always going to be little. Someday I'd be as big and tough as my brothers and cousins. I just had to be patient."

"Did you get big enough?"

"You bet." He looked into her bright eyes. "When someone runs away from home, they're usually running from something or to something." He paused. "What are you running to, Sadie?"

She shrugged.

"No." He shook his head. "Don't do that. Tell me. It's just you and me."

She scooted closer and whispered, "I have to find my daddy so he can come home and tell my mom he's sorry for hitting her."

Cheyenne gasped behind them. She sat by Sadie and gathered her into her arms. "Baby, I told you Daddy died. He's not coming back."

"But…but…you only said that 'cause he was mean to you," Sadie blubbered.

"No, baby, Daddy died."

Sammie whimpered behind her, and Cheyenne enfolded both girls as close to her as she could get them. Again, turmoil was etched across her beautiful face. He felt his heart contract. So much pain and they were still suffering. He should get up and walk away. This was none of his business, but something held him there.

He cleared his throat. "Where is your husband buried?"

"Uh…" Her watery green eyes stared at him. "In Billings. The aunt who raised him lives there and it was her wish."

"Have the girls been to his grave?" He didn't know why he was persisting. He should be halfway home by now.

"No," she replied, her frosty voice signaling for him to butt out.

He ignored the warning. "It might help."

She glared at him.

Sadie raised her head. "Does Daddy have a grave like Grandma?"

"Baby…"

"Is his name on it like Grandma's?"

Cheyenne swallowed, clearly torn by the questions.

"It might help," he repeated.

"Mr. Hart, don't you have to leave?"

"No, Mommy. He has to go with us to Daddy's grave."

That threw him, but he knew one thing: Sadie was searching for answers, and she'd somehow connected getting those answers to him. It was about time to start his day and he should be at the ranch. Yet, he stayed.

"Sadie, calm down and we'll talk about this."

But Sadie wouldn't be deterred. "Where's Daddy's grave, Mommy?"

Cheyenne sighed, giving in to the inevitable. "I'll get my jacket."

Sadie and Sammie huddled together, their arms locked around each other. They looked so sad and once again his heart contracted. He got to his feet, not sure whether to go or to stay.

Cheyenne came out the door shrugging into a brown wool jacket, a purse in her hand. "Let's go."

Sadie jumped to her feet and took his hand.

Cheyenne frowned. "Mr. Hart has work to do."

"He has to go," Sadie insisted.

He reached for his cell in his jacket pocket. "I'll let Ace know I'll be late."

Cheyenne didn't say anything. She walked to a dark blue Jeep Durango parked in the driveway and opened a back door. He noticed two car seats. The girls hurried and climbed into their seats. Cheyenne buckled Sammie in, and he went around to the passenger side and did the same for Sadie. Crawling into the front passenger seat, he realized he had a problem. The SUV was small, and he had to adjust the seat as far back as it would go to fit his long frame inside.

The interior was small, too. Only the console was between them. He could have actually reached out and touched the angry lines of Cheyenne's face. She was upset with him. That was obvious.

He removed his wool cap and gloves and stuffed them into his pocket. He felt out of place in sweats. A hat and boots would do a lot for his confidence. As she drove out of the driveway, he noticed her white-knuckling the steering wheel. She was nervous and afraid. He was sure she had her reasons for not taking the girls to their father's funeral. He should have respected that and kept his mouth shut. But he would see this through to the end, hoping she wouldn't hate him forever.

CHEYENNE DROVE STEADILY toward Billings, trying to ignore the man sitting next to her. The SUV was small, though she never realized how small until Tuf's six-foot-plus frame was within touching distance. His outdoorsy, masculine scent was appealing, but she wasn't in a mood to be tempted.

She was in a mood to smack him.

How did this happen? One minute she was frantically searching for Sadie and the next she was taking her girls to see their father's grave. When Ryan had committed suicide, she'd been devastated. After the horror and the grief, her only thought was to protect her girls.

Sadie and Sammie chatted to each other like they always did, and she tried to relax.

Tuf leaned over and whispered, "It will be okay."

She glanced at him briefly. "You don't know that."

"Evidently they didn't attend their father's funeral."

"No. They were three years old and I thought it was best. I didn't want them to have those kinds of memories of Ryan."

"Kids are very resilient."

"How many kids do you have?" she asked, not bothering to hide her annoyance at his interference.

"None. But it doesn't take someone with kids to see something is bothering Sadie."

She clenched her hands on the steering wheel and forced herself to relax, which was almost impossible. Why couldn't Tuf stay out of her life? "I've done everything to protect them," she found herself saying and didn't understand why she was explaining anything to him. "But it hasn't helped. Sadie keeps running away, and Sammie is clingy and cries all the time. I had no idea Sadie was trying to find her father."

"That's why seeing his grave will help."

"You don't know that. It could make it worse, and if it does, I'm going to blame you."

"I have broad shoulders."

"I've noticed." The words slipped out before she could stop them.

His brown eyes caught hers, and her heart raced as traitorous feminine emotions blindsided her. Damn!

"Mommy," Sadie called. "Can we get flowers like we get for Grandma's grave?"

"Sure, baby."

She negotiated traffic and pulled into a grocery store she knew carried flowers. Her hand shook as she reached for her purse. Damn him!

Tuf stretched his legs while they went inside. The girls argued over the flowers. Sadie wanted red tulips and Sammie wanted yellow. She bought both colors to save time. They ran outside to show Tuf their treasures. He seemed genuinely interested as he helped to buckle them into their seats.

Nothing was said as she drove to the cemetery, and she liked it that way. She drove through the double arcs and parked to the side as she neared the grave. Her stomach formed into a knot like it always did when she came here, reminding her of the hopes and the dreams that had died with Ryan.

Tuf stood by the car as they made their way to the site. Sadie and Sammie clutched their flowers. The dry winter lawn was neatly kept, some lingering snow nestled against the bottom of the headstone, and the flowers Cheyenne had put there at Christmas looked faded. She didn't visit the grave much because the girls, mostly Sammie, became upset if Cheyenne was out of their sight. But they'd fallen asleep while Christmas shopping in Billings, and Cheyenne had hurriedly bought and put the flowers on the grave. She felt she needed to at the holidays.

She squatted and had to swallow before she could speak. "This is where your daddy is buried. See—" she pointed to the headstone "—there's his name."

Both girls leaned in close to her, not saying anything, and she feared this was a bad idea. She had to swallow again. "Go ahead, put your flowers by the red ones."

To Cheyenne's surprise, Sammie was the first to act as she gently laid her yellow tulips by the poinsettias. Sadie was always the leader, but today she held back. Cheyenne waited, not wanting to push her. Slowly Sadie moved forward and placed her flowers by Sammie's.

"Do you have any questions?" she asked once Sadie was back in her arms.

Sadie twisted her hands. "Daddy's dead?"

Cheyenne tightened her arm around her. "Yes, baby."

"Did he love us?"

"Oh, yes. You were the light in his eyes."

"Did he love you, Mommy?"

Her throat went dry and words were now an effort. For her girls, though, she had to answer. "Yes, but Daddy was sick, and he said and did things he didn't mean."

"He's not sick no more?"

"No, baby, Daddy is at peace."

Tears rolled from Sadie's eyes and she started to cry. Sammie joined in and Cheyenne held them close. "It's okay. It's okay," she cooed.

Suddenly Sadie tore away from her and ran to Tuf, who was leaning against the car with his sneakers crossed at the ankles, observing the whole scene. Sadie took his hand and led him to the grave.

Looking up at Tuf, Sadie asked, "What's your name?"

"Tuf," he replied.

Sadie pointed to the headstone. "My daddy is dead."

Tuf squatted beside Sadie. "I know. Now you don't have to search for him anymore. You know where he is."

"Right there." Sadie pointed again.

"Yep. Do you want to say something to him?"

Sadie twisted her hands again. "L-like what?"

"I love Daddy," Sammie said.

"I love Daddy, too," Sadie added.

Tuf stood. "Tell him goodbye and we'll go get ice cream."

"Goodbye, Daddy," they chorused, and ran to the car.

Cheyenne got to her feet and Tuf reached out to help her. She didn't pull away or act insulted. "Thank you," she said. "I just never realized they needed to see their father's grave. I thought I made the right decision at the time but…"

"Don't try to second-guess yourself. Let's just hope Sadie doesn't run away anymore. Now, let's get ice cream."

"Do you know what time it is?"

"When you do something out of the ordinary, ice cream makes it that much more fun."

"Really?"

"Yes."

As they walked to the car, Cheyenne knew that Tuf Hart was a very nice man. She'd probably known that from the first day she'd met him—back in school many years ago.

But he was a man who took control—like he had today, not giving her much choice in the situation. That brought back painful memories of Ryan. He had controlled every facet of their lives, even choosing the color scheme and the furniture for their home. Her opinions didn't count.

If she'd learned anything from her disastrous marriage, it was that she'd never let another man control her.

And that included Tuf Hart.

Chapter Six

It was after ten when Tuf hurried through the back door. He heard a vacuum cleaner in another part of the house and darted up the stairs for a shower and a change of clothes. As the warm water ran over his body, his thoughts turned to Cheyenne and the hell she was going through and the hell she'd lived through.

PTSD was common among the soldiers returning from Iraq and Afghanistan. Killing and watching people being killed was a nightmare in itself. His counselor had encouraged him to talk about the nightmares, his feelings, and to get them out into the open. Keeping the horrific details of battle bottled up inside was a recipe for disaster. Soon they would bubble to the surface and destroy and disable a man more than the war. That's the reason Tuf had opened up to his family. He had to get all the pain and anguish out of his system, as his counselor had advised.

But it would never truly be out of his system. It was there lurking beneath his thoughts of family and home, making an appearance like a coward in the dead of night when his defenses were down. Then moments of horror would vividly flash before his eyes, and he'd bolt awake screaming, fighting for a way to survive.

He picked up his Silver Star from the dresser and tucked

it into his jeans. He never understood his need to keep the medal close. The counselor had said there was nothing wrong with that as long as he talked about it. He wished his mother had taken it, then he wouldn't cling to it like a baby to a pacifier. Or some such crap.

With a sigh, he jerked on his boots and wondered about Ryan. Was he one of the marines who couldn't share or talk about his experiences and in the end they had destroyed him? He'd taken his frustration out on Cheyenne. How often did he hit her? A shudder ran through Tuf as he slipped into a clean shirt. He prayed he never slid that far into the nightmare. Cheyenne and the girls deserved better. They deserved happiness.

And, once again, he was getting in too deep. Concerned. Caring. Worried. When he himself was loaded down like a U-Haul truck with life's problems.

In the hospital in Maryland, the counselor kept throwing the same question at him. "Your family is waiting in Montana, yet you're here helping a fellow marine. How does that make you feel?"

"Like hell," he'd muttered.

Honor and loyalty had kept him there. Didn't mean he didn't want to leave. He'd made it to the front door several times. He'd always turned back. Those two years had taken a toll on his emotions, but in other ways it had helped. He'd been forced to see a counselor, forced to talk, forced to open up. If he hadn't, he probably would have turned out like Ryan, keeping all the garbage inside.

But he could never see himself taking his life. He'd never do that to his mother or his family. Life to him was living, and he planned to do that the best he could manage. And if he could see Cheyenne occasionally, well, life would be like winning a gold buckle every day.

He dreamed big.

TUF STROLLED TO THE OFFICE. Hearing voices, he made his way to a corral on the other side of the main barn. Colt, Beau and Royce leaned on the pipe fence, watching Ace with a brown-and-white paint. Ace was well-known for his horse-whispering skills.

He had a bridle on the young gelding and was speaking softly to him. Every now and then the horse would rear his head, resisting.

Tuf leaned on the fence next to Colt.

"You keeping banking hours these days?" Colt asked.

"Yeah," Beau added, "I've already fed the bulls and the cows."

"Sorry, I got hung up." Tuf was glad his family wasn't treating him differently. That day in the barn when he'd spilled his guts was probably on their minds, but they never let it show.

"How do you get hung up on a run?" Colt asked.

"Someone needed help."

Beau looked at him. "Was that someone a woman?"

"Yep."

Colt slapped him on the back. "Every single woman within a hundred-mile radius is going to be after you."

"I can handle that." He grinned. But there was only one woman he wanted. Yet Cheyenne seemed a little distant on the return to Roundup. The girls chatted incessantly, and he wasn't sure if Cheyenne was still upset with him or not. Seeing Cheyenne might not be as easy as he'd like.

He turned his attention to his older brother. "Ace trying to break the horse?"

"Yeah, but the horse is nervous and temperamental. Ace is working his magic."

Just then the horse flung his head and jerked away from Ace, trotting to a corner of the corral. Ace walked over to them.

"I left this one too long. I should have been working with him months ago, but I had too much to do."

"No worry, big brother," Tuf said. "I'll break him the old-fashioned way."

"You need to save that vim and vigor for the rodeo," Ace told him.

"What better way than to start now?"

Ace narrowed his eyes. "You serious?"

"Yep."

Ace looked from the horse to Tuf. "Well, I need to be in my office, so go right ahead."

"Hot damn. It's rodeo time." Colt sailed over the fence and Beau followed. They managed to herd the horse into a chute, but the horse was frightened, nervous, jumping, throwing up his head, desperately trying to get out.

Tuf climbed the chute. "Easy, boy, easy."

Royce reached for the reins that were hanging to the ground. "Okay, Tuf. When you're ready."

Tuf eased over the railing and slid onto the horse's back. Powerful muscles rippled beneath him. He anchored his hat and reached for the reins. "Okay," he shouted. "Open the chute."

Colt and Beau swung it wide, and the horse leaped out and bucked with a force Tuf had forgotten. He found himself on the ground, staring up at a blue, blue sky.

"Damn, Tuf." He heard Colt's amused voice. "If you can't do any better than that, you're not going to make a dime."

Tuf staggered to his feet and picked up his hat lying in

the dirt. He dusted it off and slapped it onto his head. "Get him back in the chute. This isn't over."

"You're a glutton for punishment," Ace said from the sidelines.

Colt and Beau hurried the horse into the chute before he could break free. Tuf crawled onto the fence and eased onto the horse's back again. Royce handed him the reins.

"Open the chute."

The gate banged against the chute and the horse burst out like a rocket from a launchpad. Tuf held on for about two seconds before he found himself in the dirt again.

Laughter echoed on the sidelines. Leah, Flynn and his mother had joined the group.

"Tomas Hart, what are you doing?"

For the first time in his life, he ignored his mother. Well, maybe not the first. There were a couple of other times he pretended not to hear. He signaled to Colt and Beau to put the horse back in the chute. They shook their heads but did as he requested.

His body felt tight and achy, but he climbed onto that horse one more time. He was ready for the surge of power and stayed on as the horse bucked, twisted and did everything he could to get Tuf off his back. Finally, the horse galloped around the pen.

"Open the paddock gate," he yelled.

Colt ran and swung it wide. The horse bolted through with Tuf on his back. Sensing freedom, the paint's hooves slammed against the dirt and charged full speed ahead. Wet and sweaty, the horse's flowing mane slung droplets against Tuf's face. Just as Tuf decided to pull the reins, the horse stopped along Thunder Creek, breathing deeply.

Tuf stroked the wet neck. "Easy, boy, easy. We can either be friends or enemies. I prefer friends." The paint snorted and trotted to the creek to suck in water.

Tuf gave him time, talking soothingly to him, something he'd learned from Ace. After a few minutes, the horse raised his head and Tuf turned him from the creek. "Let's go home, boy."

Slowly the paint picked his way through the winter grasses and spruces. Tuf liked the horse. He had speed like Tuf had never seen. Maybe he came from racing stock. Since Sundance was getting older, he'd talk to Ace about making the horse his own.

Tuf guided the paint into the corral without incident. The guys must have been watching for him because they came out. Beau closed the gate and Tuf slid to the ground. The horse didn't move.

Colt climbed onto the fence. "I thought he'd come back alone and we'd have to go looking for you."

"I was worried about that, too," Tuf replied. "That's why I didn't get off of him in the pasture." He stroked the paint's face. "What are your plans for him, Ace?"

"He came with a group of mares Mom and I bought. I just wanted to get him broke before too much more time passed."

"I'd like him."

"Sure. He doesn't come from bucking stock, so we don't plan to use him for rodeos."

"He's fast and I like that. I'm calling him Ready to Run. I'll rub him down and feed him. Later this afternoon I'll try to put a saddle on him."

Tuf worked with the horse the rest of the day, and by the end of the week, he had Ready trained to a saddle. The more he worked with the animal, the more he felt Ready came from quarter-horse stock. He instinctively responded around cattle and he wasn't frightened of a rope.

After Ready was fully broken, Tuf turned his attention to the rodeo. They were headed to Bozeman, Montana, in a week with a load of stock for a rodeo. Tuf, Colt and Beau were scheduled to ride. They'd be away overnight, so they were taking Colt's Airstream trailer.

Tuf continued to run every morning, but he hadn't seen Cheyenne or the girls. The place was always dark when he passed by. This morning there was a light on, and since he had more nerve than common sense, he jogged down the driveway, up the steps and knocked on the door.

CHEYENNE WAS BUSY GLUING stones onto a cuff bracelet. She could get a lot done before the girl's woke up. Designing and making cowgirl jewelry was her livelihood now. She had her own website and advertised at rodeos and craft stores. Clunky bling was in, and she had several orders to fill before the twins demanded her attention.

She jumped at the knock at the door. Who could that be? It wasn't even six yet. Her dad had gone out to check on a mare that was about to foal. The knock came again. She got to her feet and tightened the belt of her green chenille robe. She hadn't combed her hair, so she tucked it behind her ears and trudged to the door in the bright psychedelic-green fuzzy slippers the girls had gotten her for Christmas. They actually glowed in the dark.

"Who is it?" she asked.

"Tuf."

Tuf? What was he doing here? She was a mess, with no makeup and her ever-present nemesis, the dreaded freckles, skimming across her nose and cheeks. She couldn't see him like this.

"It's Tuf," he called as if she hadn't heard him.

She sighed, knowing she had no choice. She smoothed her flyaway curls. He might as well see the real Cheyenne: the anxious, stressed mother of two active, fatherless little girls. Most days she didn't have time to put on lipstick, so what did she care if Tuf saw her looking less than her best? Oh, yeah, that might get her a time-out in her daughters' tell-no-lies world.

"Cheyenne."

Leaning her head against the door, she counted to ten. Maybe he'd go away. Austin had told her about Tuf's bravery in Afghanistan and it hadn't surprised her. She already knew he was that kind of man. She hoped he was seeing someone to talk about his experiences. PTSD would destroy him otherwise.

"Cheyenne."

Good grief! The man was tenacious. She opened the door, trying to hide behind it as much as she could.

His eyes slid over her disheveled appearance. "Sorry. Did I wake you?"

"No, I was working. Is there a reason you stopped by?"

"I wanted to check on Sadie."

"She's fine, and she hasn't run away again."

The cold air wafted through the door, and he looked beyond her to the fire in the living area. "May I come in?"

No. No. No! But she realized that reaction was a little insane. She stepped aside. "Would you like some coffee?" She marched into the kitchen, uncaring of what she looked like. Almost.

"Love the slippers," he said, following her.

She poured him a mug. "They were a gift from the girls. Let's just say they like bright."

As she turned around, she saw he was staring at her jewelry-making supplies on the table. "I make cowgirl jewelry," she explained.

"Oh." He took a seat and removed his cap and gloves.

Suddenly the kitchen was too small, too hot and way too intimate. Strong male vibes seemed to close in on her, reminding her that she was young and not immune to the male species. And Tuf Hart was all male.

She placed the mug in front of him with a shaky hand and slid into her chair. Picking up the leather cuff, she continued to glue the flat rhinestones around the edges.

"What is that?" he asked.

"It's a cuff made out of leather, conchas and rhinestones. I also make a light metal cuff and add whatever a woman wants."

"And women wear this?"

"Yes."

He fingered a reddish necklace lying on the table. It had five rows of red coral teardrop beads interwoven with silver spacers and pink feathers. A rhinestone boot decorated with the teardrop beads hung from it. "And this?"

"Yes."

"It looks big."

"Women like big and bold." She turned the laptop on the table so he could see her website. "The bigger pieces are my most popular items."

"Cheyenne Designs. Nice. Do you sell mostly online?"

"At Austin's store, a couple more stores in Billings and at rodeos."

He picked up a pair of round-nose pliers. 'What do you do with these?

"I use them to bend jewelry wire, make eye loops, P loops, wrapped loops and all sorts of things." She pointed to other tools on the table. "That's a cup bur for rounding the end of cut wire, and that's a flush cutter for cutting wire and—"

"Okay. I get it." He wrapped his hand around the mug, and she marveled how the mug seemed to disappear in his strong grasp. "Did you do this when Ryan was alive?"

His question startled her and she paused, laying the cuff

carefully on the table. That was really none of his business, but she supposed he was only curious and didn't mean anything by it. And she could be a little touchy about the subject. She was willing to admit that.

She folded her hands in her lap. "Not at first. Both of us were eager to start a family, and Ryan wanted me to be a stay-at-home mom. I couldn't get pregnant, and Ryan..."

"Blamed you."

She caught his brown gaze, and a shiver ran through her. Was he psychic? "Yes. But we both saw a doctor and were told we were fine and we had to be patient. It wasn't long after that I became pregnant but I...I miscarried at three months."

"And Ryan blamed you for that, too?"

She balled her hands into fists and wanted to reach across the table and smack him with one. "I'm not discussing my marriage."

He quirked an eyebrow. "They say talking is good. I've had every snippet of my life pulled out of me by a compassionate psychologist with the insights of Dr. Phil and the patience of Mother Teresa."

"I'm glad you got help. Ryan resisted every step of the way."

"It's not easy opening up and revealing painful things."

She reached for a loose rhinestone on the table. Something in the way he said that made her curious. "You know what happened to Ryan?"

"Yes."

She didn't look at him. She kept playing with the shiny stone.

"And you know what happened to me?" he asked so low she almost didn't catch the words.

"Yes. It's hard to keep secrets when our families are now so closely entwined."

His eyes caught hers and she couldn't look away. "I'm sorry for what you had to go through."

"And I'm sorry you had to witness so much carnage." She glimpsed a shadow of pain, which was quickly replaced by a teasing glimmer.

"So why don't you take pity on this cowboy/marine and go out with him sometime?"

She melted into his warm gaze for a second but was quickly slammed against the hard facts of reality. Ryan's suicide had crippled her emotionally. At times she felt dead all the way to her soul, and she fought that feeling for her girls. For them she went through the motions of everyday life. For them she smiled and pretended she was happy because they needed to see that. For them she would do anything to ensure their happiness.

How did she explain that to Tuf? And why did she feel she had to explain it?

"Don't say you don't like me. We both know you'd be lying."

She shrugged. "That was just a way to protect my pride," she admitted. "Our families didn't get along, and our dating would have only caused more problems."

"Problem solved. Our families have united in a way no one would have ever expected."

"It's not that simple."

"Why isn't it?"

"Because everything I do is for my girls. They're my focus, my life. I don't have time or energy for anything else."

"I understand that, but I've learned one thing from counseling—you can't keep all those emotions inside. You have to share, open up and live life. Otherwise you live in a vacuum, and that's not good for you or the girls." He blew out a breath. “And that’s the longest speech you’ll ever get from me.”

“Tuf…”

He held up a hand. “Okay. Can we be friends? Can I stop by here every now and then and have a cup of coffee? No strings. No attachment. No making out. Just friendship.”

She stared into his stubborn brown eyes. “You’re very persistent.”

He grinned and her heart hammered wildly. Oh, he was good.

“My dad used to say I was like an old hound dog with a juicy bone. I could never let go of anything.”

“I hope I’m not a juicy bone.” She tried very hard not to smile, but she felt the corners of her mouth twitch.

“The very best.”

As tempting as he was, she had to say no. Even though it had been more than ten years, their situation hadn’t changed much. They still weren’t right for each other. They had too much baggage and heartache to deal with. They had to conquer their demons alone.

Then he did something unexpected. He reached across the table and ran one long finger across her freckles. His touch was light and gentle. He’d never touched her before, and a sea of emotions swamped her, emotions she’d just sworn she didn’t have. Why was she suddenly hot all over and had the urge to giggle?

“In grade school, I thought your freckles were cute. I actually tried to count them one time when we sat across from each other in the cafeteria. You frowned at me, so I had to stop counting. In high school you covered them with makeup, but I like the freckles.”

Was he for real? Ryan never cared for her freckles. He preferred her in makeup.

"I'd like it if we could be friends. Do you think that's possible?"

No. No. No!

But the word that slipped from her dry mouth was "Yes."

Chapter Seven

Tuf watched the startled expression on her pretty face and wondered if she was confused by her decision to see him or guilty she'd agreed to see someone other than her deceased husband. Before she could change her mind, he said, "I've got to run. Busy day at the ra..." His words trailed away as he heard childish chatter.

"The girls are awake," Cheyenne murmured.

Two whirlwinds blew into the kitchen and abruptly stopped when they saw him. They stopped so fast Sammie ran into Sadie. They both wore one-piece pajamas. Green frogs danced on Sadie's purple ones and Sammie's were pink Barbie all the way.

Sadie's eyes opened wide. "You came to see me?"

"Sure did, munchkin. How you doing?"

"Good. Sammie's good, too."

Their red hair was everywhere, and Sammie kept brushing hers out of her eyes. Sammie whispered something in Sadie's ear.

"Sammie wants to know why you call me munchkin."

"Because you're cute and small."

Sammie whispered in Sadie's ear again.

"Sammie wants to know what you call her."

He studied Sammie's face, the same as Sadie's. "Well, I think I have two munchkins here. You're identical."

They giggled and Tuf felt like laughing, too. They were so darn cute.

Sammie whispered to Sadie again.

"Stop it, Sammie," Cheyenne said. "You can talk. Sadie doesn't need to speak for you. Now, what do you want for breakfast?"

The whispering started again as the two debated this in their own twinlike language. Finally, Sadie said, "We want pancakes."

"Go wash your hands and comb your hair," Cheyenne instructed. They darted off, but Sadie turned back. "Bye, Tuf." Their heads were together again and they could hear Sadie. "You better say it."

"Bye, Tuf," Sammie said.

"Bye," he called and then looked at Cheyenne. "Are they always like that?"

"Yes, and it gets annoying. Sadie's the dominant one and Sammie relies on her for everything."

Tuf drained his mug. "Are they in school?"

"They should be in pre-K, but after Ryan's death they were very clingy and cried all day in class so I took them out and I'm homeschooling them. When they start kindergarten, I want to separate them, but I don't know if they're ready. Sammie has to find her own identity, though."

"Since Sadie has accepted her father's death, maybe they'll both grow stronger in the months ahead."

"That's my hope."

He stood and pulled his hat and gloves out of his jacket pocket. Slipping his cap over his head, he said, "I'll see you later."

"Tuf…"

He could hear the hesitation, the fear in her voice, and

he wasn't letting her go back on her word. He leaned over and whispered in her ear, "Later." A flowery, feminine scent weakened his knees and he had trouble moving away. "Tell that to the other Cheyenne who is scared to death of life." He walked toward the door, shoving his hands into his gloves.

"I'm not scared." Her words followed him.

"Good."

"Tuf Hart..."

He closed the door and smiled as he went down the steps and all the way to Thunder Ranch. He didn't know what he expected from their friendship. All he knew was that he liked Cheyenne. He always had and he wanted to get to know her better.

She was right about one thing: they both had a lot of emotional baggage. Maybe they could work on lightening the load together or whatever. So far things were going good and he wanted to keep it that way. Friendship was a good start, but he knew and she knew that he wanted a lot more.

AS TUF HURRIED THROUGH the back door, he met his mom in her customary jeans and flannel shirt.

"Tomas." She glanced at her watch. "You're running late. We have a business meeting in ten minutes."

"I was talking to Cheyenne and..."

"Cheyenne." A sharp note ran through her otherwise calm voice. "She wouldn't go out with you in high school. The nerve! Who wouldn't want to go out with my handsome son?"

He tried not to smile at her offended expression. "Well, Mom, your handsome son's father was John Hart, and Dad didn't like Buddy's thieving ways. Do you see the conflict?"

"Yes." She shook her head. "Things sure have changed. Not sure how your father would take that, but I like Austin and I've always liked Buddy."

His mom liked everybody. That's why he was startled by her reaction to Cheyenne's name.

She looked up at him, her eyes worried. "Are you and Cheyenne friends now?"

"Yeah, we're friends."

Suddenly, she wrapped her arms around him and hugged. "I don't want anyone to hurt you ever again."

"Mom, you can't always protect me. I'm old enough to handle anything life throws at me."

She pulled back and brushed away a tear. Sharp, needle-like pains shot through his stomach.

"We can talk about Afghanistan if you want to." Since that day in the barn, she hadn't mentioned it, and she seemed to purposefully avoid the subject.

"Why would I bring up that subject? I do not want you to relive any of it."

But I do. In the darkest of night.

"I'm fine, Mom." He felt he needed to reassure her. "I've checked in with the VA in Billings, and I can see a counselor anytime I feel the walls closing in."

"You can talk to me, too."

"I know, Mom."

She patted his chest. "You're home now and safe. That's what matters." She reached for her Carhartt jacket on the wooden coatrack. "Do you ever hear from Michael Dobbins?"

He fished his phone out of his pocket. "I got a text from him yesterday. See." He punched a couple of buttons and showed her the message: Farmer again. Never felt so good. "Here's a picture." He brought up a photo of Michael on a tractor. "His family are farmers in Kansas."

"He looks quite normal."

"He is, except for the artificial leg and eye and numerous other scars, but he's living life again."

"All because of you."

Tuf swallowed, not really wanting to talk about that heartbreaking time or take credit for it, but he'd encouraged her to talk. Luckily, her cell buzzed.

She grabbed it off the counter. "Yes, Aidan, we'll be right there." Clicking off, she said, "Get dressed. I'll stall."

He ran upstairs, and in ten minutes he walked into the office, which was filled with family, even Dinah and Duke.

"Still keeping those banker hours," Colt commented.

"Shut up." Tuf grinned.

His mom started the meeting. "I won't keep everyone waiting. Josh and I have talked, and I've made a decision about Midnight. That horse has caused us so many problems that at times I wanted to strangle the poor thing. But we have a lot invested in him, and I intend to see that horse doing wonders for Thunder Ranch and Hart Rodeo Contracting Company. That's been my goal from the start."

She took a moment. "I know all of you have different opinions about Midnight's role in the rodeo. Mine has changed several times. Midnight getting injured could thwart all our plans. That's been a big factor, but Aidan has been able to collect semen from Midnight. At first, he was unable to do this because the animal was too unpredictable, and we didn't want Aidan or a handler getting hurt." She looked around the room. "So I've decided to enter Midnight in rodeos to see if he can live up to his reputation as an exceptional bareback bronc."

"Hot damn." Colt raised a fist in the air. "Time to rodeo."

"Colton." His mother's stern voice brought Colt down

to earth quickly. "It will be your job to keep Midnight as calm as possible and living up to his potential."

"Yes, ma'am."

Everyone got up from their seats, preparing to leave.

"Wait a minute," Dinah called. "I have news."

Now everyone stared at her, and she rose to her feet, her hand on her stomach. "Austin and I found out that we're having a…girl. We're so excited."

Everyone jockeyed for a position to hug her.

"Another granddaughter," Sarah cried, squeezing the daylights out of her daughter. "How wonderful. They'll grow up as best friends."

Tuf was the last to hug her. "How are you going to handle your sheriffing duties while—" he glanced at her rounded stomach "—you're pregnant?"

"I got the okay to hire another full-time deputy, and I'm on office duty for now."

"What a relief." Sarah sighed.

The family dispersed to start their day. Tuf helped Beau feed the rodeo bulls. He brushed hay from his clothes and watched the bulls tearing into the alfalfa.

"That brown-and-red one looks mean."

Beau leaned on the fence beside him. "That's Bushwhacker and he is mean. His main goal is to gore you as soon as he can. I drew him once. Didn't make the ride, and I got the hell out of his way as fast as I could."

"That's what I like about horses. Once the ride is over, they're searching for the open gate to get out of the arena. They're not looking to maim you for life."

"I just like riding bulls."

"Well, coz, let's see how we do in the next few months, and hopefully we make it home in one piece."

Later that afternoon, Tuf worked with Ready. The horse rode as smooth as Mrs. Worley's Cadillac. Brad, her son, had been in his class, and Mrs. Worley always drove them to school outings in her big smooth-as-a-glider Cadillac. Yep, Ready was a Cadillac horse.

The cows needed hay, so he cranked up the tractor and carried a round bale of hay to them. As he worked, he thought of Cheyenne. Hell, there wasn't a minute of the day that he hadn't thought of her. Was he still infatuated with her? Or was it something more? He wasn't sure, but he was willing to find out.

THE NEXT MORNING CHEYENNE was up early, brushed her hair and clipped it back. All the while she resisted the urge to put on a touch of makeup. Tuf liked her freckles. She stopped. What was she doing? She couldn't keep saying no and feeling excited at the same time. Picking up her box of supplies, she headed for the kitchen in her first-thing-in-the-morning look.

Her dad had made a fire in the fireplace and she could smell coffee. He was an early riser, but this morning he'd gone to Thunder Ranch to check on Midnight. It was one of his favorite things.

Cheyenne fixed her coffee and laid out her supplies. She had ten sparkly stretchy bracelets in different colors to make, and she could whip them out in no time. As she worked, she kept glancing at the clock. Six-fifteen—no Tuf. Six-thirty—no knock on the door. By seven, she knew he wasn't stopping to visit.

Finishing the bracelets, she placed them in a small box and stored them inside her big box, trying to figure out why she felt hurt. She liked Tuf, even his weird shopping habits. She liked his compassion for her girls, his selfless bravery and his inherent strength. But after what she'd been through with Ryan, she wasn't ready for any kind of intimate relationship, even if Tuf was charming, caring and unbelievably heart-stoppingly good-looking.

"Oh, oh," she groaned. She needed something stronger than coffee to deal with her unsettling thoughts. Getting up, she stood on tiptoes to reach the top cabinet door. She pulled out a bowl of candy—the girls' stash that she gave them when they were good.

Tootsie Rolls, M&M'S, bubble gum, Dots, gummy bears, Twix and Milky Ways. She grabbed a Milky Way, tore off the wrapper and took a bite. Oh, yeah, just what she needed. Almost.

After her sugar high, she put Tuf out of her mind. They'd agreed to be friends, and anything else was out of the question. That was her bottom line and she was sticking to it.

The next morning she heard his knock and calmly walked to the door and opened it, uncaring of her gaudy robe and slippers.

Tuf brought the cool outdoors in with him. He removed his gloves and held his hands to the fire.

"I need new gloves. I think I've worn these out. Feel." He cupped her face with his hands and she lost all train of thought. The roughened male skin against her soft face shot her adrenaline through the roof. She knew he intended to show her how cold his hands were, but all she felt was warmth all the way to her toes. His dark eyes stared into hers, and the world stopped turning for a brief moment as she realized just how much she liked Tuf Hart. *Friends.* She kept trying to remind herself. Friends wasn't even on her radar. Friends with benefits wasn't even an option. How did she get from *no* to the delicious thoughts in her head?

She hated that he could make her so wishy-washy when she intended to be firm in her decision.

"W-would you like a cup of coffee?"

"As long as it's hot."

He followed her into the kitchen and sank into a chair. "Making jewelry, huh?"

"Yes."

He stared at her. "You seem tense."

"I want to make it clear that we're just friends."

"Okay." His gaze grew intense. "Something else is bothering you."

"Yes, it's about the cemetery the other day. I should have mentioned it sooner, but you put me in a difficult position. I make all decisions concerning my girls, and I do not appreciate you taking control."

His eyes narrowed. "Did something happen?"

"No, except they want to go to the grave site every day. I told them it was too far and we'd go once a month. We circled a date on the calendar. They haven't mentioned it since."

"So?"

She could see the confusion on his handsome face. She placed a cup of coffee in front of him and slid into a chair feeling foolish. Ridiculously foolish. Before she knew what she was doing, she started telling him about her marriage and Ryan. She didn't sugarcoat anything.

"Ryan was a control freak in every way and it only grew worse."

"Did you ever think of leaving him?"

"He was in so much pain I couldn't bring myself to do that until...until one day he became enraged that I hadn't taken his clothes to the cleaners. Sammie had the flu and I wasn't taking her out. He hit me so hard I fell in the kitchen and hit my head on the table. Blood ran into my eyes, and I knew one of us had to leave or he was going to kill me. I told him to get out and not to return until he got some help. I thought he was going to hit me again, but he walked out. That was the last I saw him." She gripped her hands until her knuckles were white. "It breaks my heart that Sadie saw that."

"She just wanted her daddy to say he was sorry so he could come home."

"I know but…"

"Sadie will be fine." Then he told her the story about the little girl in Afghanistan. "The girl went through a horrific event, but the moment she saw her toy, the horror was forgotten."

"That's why you were so stern that day you saw Sadie walking on the road?"

"Yeah."

She stared into his brown eyes and saw a vortex of dark emotions that still lingered from the war. But he wasn't trying to hide them like Ryan had.

Suddenly the darkness faded. "I'm not trying to control you, Cheyenne. I'm really not that type. I was just trying to help Sadie."

Seeing the turmoil on his face, she knew she had to be honest. "I'm a mess. My emotions are helter-skelter, and I do my best to get through each day for my girls. But—" she shifted uneasily "—earlier when you cupped my face, I felt warm and feminine again."

"Is there something wrong with that?"

"Yes. I'm an emotional wreck, and I'm finding every excuse I can to stay away from you."

"Well, then, stop nailing up excuses like barbed wire to keep me away. Let's just take this one day at a time. What do you say?"

She licked her dry lips. "Tuf…why would you want to do that? I can't see any kind of future for us. We both have too much baggage."

He twisted his cup. "But there's an attraction between us. It's been there since we were teenagers." He looked directly at her, and his dark eyes were as inviting as the chocolate on a Milky Way bar. "Can you deny that?"

"No, but I'm scared." Oh, God! Had she said that out loud?

"I know. I am, too."

His honesty startled her, and she just stared at him, all her defenses down. But she didn't feel weak or vulnerable. She was uplifted knowing she wasn't alone in her fears.

"Is it okay if I continue to stop by?"

"Yes," she replied, and meant it.

"Tuf," Sadie screeched from the doorway and jumped onto Tuf's lap. "You came to see me again?"

"Yep. How you doing?" He cradled her close as if he'd been doing it all his life.

"Good." Sadie bobbed her head.

Cheyenne wondered where Sammie was. The girls were inseparable. She stood to go check when a loud scream was followed by wails. "Mommy! Mommy!" She sprinted to their room and found Sammie standing in the middle of Sadie's bed crying her little heart out.

"Baby, it's okay. Mommy's here." She gathered her child into her arms.

"Sadie left me." Sammie hiccuped. "I'm scared."

"Mommy's here. There's nothing to be afraid of." She reached for tissues on the nightstand between the beds and wiped Sammie's wet face. The girls had twin beds, but Sammie always crawled into Sadie's during the night. At times like this, Cheyenne became so angry at Ryan for doing this to his kids.

She carried Sammie to the kitchen, and Sammie was on full attack as they often were when the girls were mad at each other. "You left me, Sadie."

"I had to say hi to Tuf."

"I want to say hi to Tuf," Sammie mumbled.

Cheyenne stood her on her feet, and she climbed onto Tuf's other leg, but her attention was on her sister. "You left me."

"You're a big baby," Sadie spat.

"Am not." Sammie slapped her sister's chest.

Sadie hit her back. "Am, too."

"No hitting," Cheyenne said. "Now make up."

"She's a big baby," Sadie insisted, resisting, as always.

"You're mean!" Sammie cried.

"Girls, did you not hear what I said? Make up and be nice."

They glared at her and then at each other. Slowly their foreheads met and they started to whisper. Tuf rolled his eyes over their heads, and Cheyenne smiled, feeling lighthearted and silly. She hadn't felt that way in a long time.

"I've got to go to work, girls," Tuf announced, and they scrambled from his lap, staring up at him.

"When you coming back?" Sadie asked.

The back door opened, and Cheyenne's dad stomped in, wiping snow from his boots. He stopped short in the doorway. "Tuf." A startled expression flashed across his face.

Tuf walked over and the two men shook hands. "Mornin', Buddy."

"Mornin'. I was just at Thunder Ranch exercising Midnight."

"Gracie said you took care of him when he went missing."

"Yeah. Grew kind of fond of the horse."

"You're welcome anytime. Now I've got to run," Tuf said and looked at her. "See you later."

She nodded and wondered if she was just weak or if she was glimpsing a light through the darkness that surrounded her heart.

The girls ran behind him to the door. "Bye, Tuf," they called and then ran to the bathroom to get ready for breakfast.

"Tuf Hart?" Her dad lifted a shaggy eyebrow when the door closed.

"Take that pained look off your face. We're just friends."

He poured a cup of coffee. "Mmm. I'm glad he helped with Sadie. We didn't know what else to do."

"I'm grateful for that, too." Her conflicting thoughts she kept to herself.

He sipped his coffee. "Just take it slow. Tuf's been through a war, and you've been battered and bruised."

Her dad rarely offered parental advice. He figured he'd lost that right many years ago, so for him to speak up she knew he was worried.

She kissed his cheek. "Dad..."

"I just don't want to ever see you like you were when you came home over a year ago—totally defeated and withdrawn."

She didn't, either. She wouldn't survive another debilitating heartache like that. "I'm taking baby steps," she told him. "I better check on the girls."

As she walked toward the bathroom, she felt Tuf's hands cupping her face. Why was that feeling so strong?

Chapter Eight

Tuf and Beau checked Tuf's rigging for bareback riding. They sat at Beau's workstation in the barn next to the old foreman's house. Beau had converted the small barn into a saddlery. A gorgeous saddle Beau had just finished sat on a large sawhorse. The scent of leather filled the room and cuttings lay on the floor.

They examined the Barstow rigging that Austin had ordered for Tuf. The leather strap placed around the horse's withers had a luggagelike handle made out of rawhide. The underside was sheepskin to protect the knuckles. Slipping his gloved hand into the handle, Tuf gripped it tight.

"Just right," he said. "I have a good grip, and I can get my hand in and out without a problem."

Beau nodded. "That's why it's the best."

"I'll put it in my truck with the rest of my gear."

"Wait. I have something else for you."

Tuf walked back in, and Beau grabbed a package wrapped in brown paper. "I made this for you."

Tuf glanced at the package and then at Beau. "Now, that's too little for a saddle."

"I made you a saddle years ago."

"And I still use it." He stared at the package, wondering what was inside. For some reason he was hesitant to take it. He was sure it was something special, and guys didn't do special. They laughed, joked and horsed around. Special meant his heart was about to take a hit. That's why guys like him avoided it.

"Open it." Beau shoved it at him.

Slowly, he laid the rigging on the table and took the package. Ripping off the paper, he could only stare. He held up the item and felt his heart take a nosedive, just as he'd foreseen. Red chaps with white fringe and blue stars ran down each side—red, white and blue for an American marine.

"I don't know what to say" was all he could manage.

"If you don't like them, you don't have to wear them. I thought they would give you a brand—cowboy marine."

"They're nice, really nice. I appreciate it and I'll definitely wear them. Thanks, coz." Tuf held out his hand.

They shook hands and then did a brief hug and laughed.

"We're hopeless," Tuf said.

"Now, if you were Sierra, I'd hug you like crazy."

"Let's remember I'm not when we're sleeping in that small Airstream trailer."

"Let's go see what time Ace wants us to leave for Bozeman on Friday morning."

"Do you want to guess?" Tuf asked.

"Early."

"Yep." They walked out of the barn toward the office.

Ace wanted them on the road at six. He was staying behind to keep an eye on a mare that was showing signs of distress with her pregnancy. Since it was one of Midnight's offspring, Ace wasn't taking any chances.

Tuf had a lot to do before they left. His last rodeo had been in November, so he was a little rusty but felt his technique would come back. He intended not to think too much about it. He didn't want to leave without seeing Cheyenne and the girls.

He hated she was in so much turmoil, and he didn't want to push or control her. Her husband had really done a number on her. Tuf just wanted to help her. As Ace and Beau talked, he tried to figure out why that was so important.

IN THE LATE AFTERNOON, Tuf drove to the Wright place. Cheyenne, the girls and Buddy were at the corrals. He parked by the old tin-rusted barn and walked over.

"Tuf!" The girls squealed and ran to him.

"What's going on?"

"Grandpa bought us horses," Sadie informed him.

He took their hands and walked closer. Cheyenne smiled at him, and his heart kicked against his ribs like a bronc about to be broken. Damn, she was beautiful with the sun glistening off her hair. Today none of her angst showed on her face.

"Hi," she said in that soft voice that made his insides feel like jelly.

Before he could say anything, Buddy led the horses over. One was white with black flecks and the other a muted gold with a white blaze face.

"Hey, Tuf," Buddy said.

He nodded. "Where did you get the horses?"

"Over at Angie's animal rescue. They've got some age on 'em and are gentle. I thought they'd be perfect for the girls."

"I don't want to ride," Sammie said, clinging to Cheyenne's leg.

"It's okay, baby. You don't have to," Cheyenne told her.

Sadie climbed onto the fence. "I'm gonna ride."

"Since Sammie's not, you get to choose," Buddy said to Sadie. "Which horse do you want?"

Sadie shrugged.

"Come on, munchkin," Tuf urged. "Which one do you like?"

"That one." She pointed to the gold one.

Buddy tied the white horse to the fence and led the gold horse closer. A child's saddle was on both horses. "You ready?"

Sadie looked at her mother, then at Tuf and back at the horse. Her eyes flickered with uncertainty. "Come with me, Tuf."

Tuf was startled. He thought Sadie would want her mother to ride with her because Cheyenne was an expert horsewoman. But with Sammie attached to her leg, she could barely move.

He looked at Cheyenne for approval. He wasn't doing anything without her okay. That lesson he'd already learned.

"Baby, are you sure?" she asked Sadie.

"Yep." Sadie bobbed her head. "If Tuf helps me."

"Okay," Cheyenne said.

He leaped over the fence and then plucked Sadie off her perch. "Let's get acquainted with… What are you going to name her?"

Sadie shook her head.

Tuf stroked the horse's face and Sadie tentatively stuck out her hand. "Don't be afraid," he said. "I'm here."

She touched the face and then started petting in earnest. "See, she likes me."

"Yes, she does," he agreed and wondered how old the animal was. She seemed almost sedated, which worked well for a scared little girl.

"Now I'm going to put you in the saddle, and I'll swing up behind you. Okay?"

"'Kay."

"But first we have to give her a name."

Sadie looked at Cheyenne and then at Buddy. "Grandpa, what's her name?"

"She's just an old horse without a name. You have to give her one."

"'Kay." She touched the horse's face. "I wanna call her Tuf."

"Sadie, baby, you have to give her another name. That's Tuf's name."

He glanced at Cheyenne and saw she was smiling. He was smiling, too. He'd never been around kids that much and found he liked it, especially Cheyenne's girls.

"I wanna call her Tuf," she insisted with a stubborn lift of her chin.

"How about if we call her Toughie?" he suggested.

"'Kay. I'm gonna ride Toughie."

"Here we go." Tuf lifted her into the saddle and held on in case Sadie started screaming. She gripped the saddle horn with both hands but didn't make a sound. He adjusted the stirrup to her leg length and slipped her purple boot in. He didn't have to look to know that Sammie's cowgirl boots were pink.

Buddy adjusted the other side and Tuf swung up behind Sadie. Buddy handed him the reins.

"How do we start her, Tuf?" she asked.

He suppressed a laugh. "Like this." He kneed the horse and was surprised when the horse actually moved. He could have sworn he heard a snore. They trotted around the corral and Sadie finally let go of the saddle horn. He showed her how to use the reins and she caught on quickly.

"Look, Mommy, I'm riding."

Sammie had finally let go of Cheyenne's leg, and they had climbed the fence to watch. "I see, baby."

Sadie pulled up the horse and turned to look at him. "I can drive by myself now."

"No," Cheyenne was quick to say.

"I can do it by myself," Sadie shouted.

"The horse barely moves, girl. She'll be fine," Buddy said to his daughter.

Indecision filtered across Cheyenne's pretty face so Tuf made it easy for her. He slid to the ground. "Go slow," he instructed in a stern voice. Around and around the corral Sadie guided the horse, even being bold enough to stand in the stirrups. He followed her on one side, and Buddy was on the other just in case she took a tumble. When it was clear Sadie had it mastered, he strolled over to Cheyenne.

"I can't believe she learned so quickly."

Tuf pushed back his hat. "Look who her mother is."

She smiled, and he couldn't look away from the light in her green eyes. "That was a long time ago."

He pointed to the barrels outside the fence. "They're getting rusty. You might spray paint them and see what Sadie can do."

"I don't think she's ready for that."

"Sammie," Sadie called. "Ride with me. It's fun."

Sammie's eyes were glued on her twin. Tuf saw the fear in her eyes and knew that was the worst feeling in the world. He'd felt it many times. Mostly when high-powered bullets were whizzing past his helmet or when he had to tell a wounded buddy that everything was going to be okay when in truth he was scared out of his mind. There was only one way to conquer fear—to not let it have control. Sammie was only four, but the fear was just as real.

He walked to the white horse and led her over. "This is your horse. Do you want to pet her?"

Sammie's eyes opened wide and Tuf glanced at Cheyenne. She nodded.

"Does she bite?" Sammie asked, shocking both adults.

"Um...no," he said with certainty. He wasn't sure the horse was even breathing much less have enough energy to injure someone.

"Her name is Princess," Sammie announced, shocking them again.

Tuf lifted the girl off the fence and felt her tremble. "You don't have to ride if you don't want to."

"I know," she replied and reached out a hand to touch the horse, and then she stroked her. "She's pretty."

"Yes, she is." He gently placed her in the saddle and waited for the crying. None came. He adjusted the stirrup and slid her pink boot in. Buddy hurried to adjust the other side.

"That's my girl." Buddy encouraged her.

Tuf swung up behind her and kneed the horse. The horse trotted off and Sammie's trembling grew severe and he held her tight. He didn't stop the horse or take her off because he knew it was important to her to do what her twin was doing. Tuf knew that feeling, too.

After about the third trip around the corral with Sadie constantly passing them, the trembling stopped. He showed her how to use the reins and she grew confident. When she looked back at him, he knew it was time to get off, which he did, but he followed along the side.

Once Sammie had it mastered and Buddy was watching both of them, Tuf walked over to Cheyenne. "You can breathe now."

"I can't believe she did that. Since Ryan...she's been so clingy and needy, but look at her." He followed her gaze to see Sammie following Sadie around the corral. "She's having fun." Her eyes caught his, and he got lost in her rapturous expression. "All because of you. Neither one of them would have gotten on a horse for Dad or me. We tend to pamper them, but they wanted to impress you."

"So they like me?"

"Yes."

He leaned on the fence about six inches from her and stared into her gorgeous eyes. "How about their mother?"

"She does, too," she whispered.

Her pink, full and inviting lips were inches away. He pressed closer, needing to breathe the same air.

"Cheyenne," Buddy called, and a curse word slid down Tuf's throat. "It's getting late. We're taking the horses in to rub them down, and Angie sent some horse cookies the girls can feed them."

"Okay, Dad."

Tuf raised a hand. "Bye, girls." He hadn't paid any attention to the time, but the sun was about to slam-dunk another day.

The girls clamored to get off and Buddy helped. In a split second they charged toward Tuf. He squatted and held out his arms to catch them. "Thank you, Tuf," they chorused.

"I'm proud of you. You both did really good."

Sadie kissed his right cheek and Sammie kissed the left. Then they ran after Buddy. Tuf swung over the fence and landed by Cheyenne.

"I'm fixing to start rodeoing so I'll be gone quite a bit. Do you mind if I call to see how the girls are doing?"

"No. They would love that." She gave him her cell number and he entered it into his phone. "My cell is at the house, but when you call I'll have your number."

He slipped his phone back into the case on his leather belt, and his eyes caught hers. The light he saw there gave him the courage to say, "When a cowboy rides away, he usually gets a kiss from a pretty cowgirl."

She lifted an eyebrow. "Are you riding away?"

"Temporarily."

'Well, then." She stood on tiptoes and gently touched his lips. He cupped her face, needing her touch, her caress a little longer. His lips took hers with the same gentleness but he was unable to disguise the fire leaping within him. He pulled away like someone who had just been given CPR. He had what he needed for now—to survive. He strolled toward his truck.

"Bye, Tuf," she called in a wistful voice.

He didn't turn back. The best was yet to come.

Chapter Nine

Cheyenne closed *Sleeping Beauty,* kissed her daughters and tucked them in for the night. Out of all the new books they had, the girls preferred her to read the classic fairy tales at night. They were from the Little Golden Books collection Cheyenne had as a child. Just like her daughters, she'd dreamed of a prince, too. That was in books, though. In the real world, a prince was very rare. Or realistic.

Flipping off the light, she watched to make sure the night-light was on, and then she went to the kitchen to prepare the girls' lesson plan for tomorrow. Her dad was asleep in his chair.

In the utility room, she pulled a box of school supplies out of a cabinet. In the morning they'd work on motor skills, and in the afternoon they'd color and read. Marbles in a jar, nuts and bolts so they could pick up and screw on, and then pipe filters and beads to make a bracelet. They'd read *The Very Hungry Caterpillar* and *If You Give a Mouse a Cookie.* That settled in her mind, she went to her bedroom to finish several jewelry orders.

But her thoughts kept straying to Tuf and the kiss. She didn't think twice about kissing him. It felt natural and right. And damn good. She'd been resisting an obvious attraction since she'd met Tuf. Placing her pliers on the table, she decided to stop resisting, to stop comparing Tuf to Ryan and to stop looking for fault where there was none. And to stop being afraid of a simple thing like falling in love. Again.

Six months ago she would have said that it wasn't even a possibility.

But now…she was starting to believe.

THE NEXT MORNING EVERYONE was up early getting ready for the trip to Bozeman. Tuf swallowed one last sip of coffee.

"Mom, you sure you're going to be okay?"

She turned from putting dishes in the dishwasher, giving him one of those looks. "Tomas Hart, I'm fine. I have my nitroglycerin pills in my pocket, in my bedroom and in the office. I wish you kids would stop worrying."

He placed his cup in the sink. "Did you ever stop worrying about me?"

"I'm your mother, and mothers never stop worrying."

He kissed her cheek. "I want you around for a long, long time."

"I don't plan on going anywhere."

"Good." He reached for his hat. "I just hate you being alone in this big house."

"If it will make you feel better, Leah and the kids are spending the night."

"Yep. That makes me happy."

She pushed him toward the door. "Now make your mama happy and focus on the rodeo."

"Yes, ma'am."

For the next hour, Ace and Colt shouted orders like drill sergeants, but everyone did his or her job without complaining. Colt backed the cattle carrier up to a chute attached to a corral. Tuf rode Ready and herded the saddle broncs into the corral and into the chute. They loaded easily, and Royce closed the first compartment gate. He did the same with the bareback horses. Beau and Gracie followed with the bulls, and they charged into the carrier without a problem.

That left Midnight to occupy the last compartment alone. Colt ushered him into the corral and managed to get him in the chute, but that's where Midnight balked. He stopped short, refusing to budge.

Colt climbed onto the pipe railing. "C'mon, boy." He rubbed Midnight's back and the horse reared his head. "C'mon, boy. You've done this before. It's rodeo time. Don't make me look like an ass."

"You don't need any help from Midnight," Ace remarked.

Colt shot him a killer glance. "C'mon, boy," he said again and slapped Midnight on the rump. The horse darted into the compartment, and Royce slammed the door closed before Midnight could change his mind.

"Let's go," Colt shouted, swinging over the fence.

Tuf hooked up to the Airstream trailer. The truck bed was loaded with hay and feed and covered with a tarp in case of rain or snow.

"Let's go," Colt shouted again.

The cattle carrier pulled away from the corral and Tuf followed. They settled in for the long ride. Country music blared on the radio. Tuf sipped his coffee and stayed as close to the cattle carrier as he could.

But his thoughts were on Cheyenne. He could see her at the kitchen table making jewelry in her green robe and bright slippers. They were friends, and slowly that friendship was developing into something more. He felt it yesterday when she'd kissed him, and he really hoped he wasn't misreading the signals. The memory of her kiss had to last for a while. That was the easy part. All he had to do was close his eyes and she was there in his arms, touching her sweet lips to his.

Beau took the wheel of Tuf's truck for the last leg of the trip. Tuf catnapped. He wasn't sure how much time had passed when Beau said, "Hey, we're heading into Bozeman."

The sign for Bozeman appeared ahead, and the right blinkers on the carrier came on.

Tuf sat up. "Everything okay?"

"Yep, except Midnight keeps staring at me."

Ever since they'd left Roundup, the horse had been watching the truck. "He's a little restless on the road."

"On the road? He's restless all the time," Beau told him.

"Yeah, Ace said they knew that when they purchased him, but they've worked wonders since then. If he doesn't perform well, though, it will be a big loss for Thunder Ranch."

"A lot rides on that horse."

"You bet."

They pulled into the fairgrounds. Colt jumped out of the carrier and walked over. He took a moment to make sure Midnight was okay.

When Colt reached Tuf, he thumbed over his shoulder. "You do realize you'll probably have to ride him one of these days."

"Yep." Tuf shoved his hat back on his head. "I'm hoping it's not this rodeo."

Colt laughed. "I'll check with the coordinator and see where we need to unload."

Tuf stretched his legs, as did Beau, who was on his cell with Sierra.

Colt came back with instructions. They unloaded Midnight in a separate pen because he was a stud and there were too many mares around. Once in the pen, he charged around the perimeter looking for a way out. When he found none, he settled down and drank from a water trough. The rest of the unloading went smoothly.

They found a spot to park and hook up the Airstream trailer. After that, they fed the animals. His mom had stocked the trailer with food, so they went back to eat and rest before the rodeo.

Bareback riding was first, and Tuf took his rodeo gear to the cowboy-ready area. Colt and Beau handled the stock.

Tuf took a moment to look out at the stands, full of eager rodeo followers. Sponsors' signs were plastered around the arena. Vendors sold hotdogs, sandwiches, cotton candy, pretzels and more. The scent of popcorn mixed with the foul odor of manure and rawhide wafted on the air.

Yep, it was a rodeo.

The press box was above the chutes, and a Garth Brooks tune played on the loudspeakers. The announcer came on and introduced the cowgirls, who were dressed in white. Circling the arena on horseback, they carried both the Montana state and U.S. flags. They formed a line in the center of the arena and stopped.

"Ladies and gentlemen—" the announcer's voice came on "—please stand for the national anthem. Our own Marsha Gates will sing it."

Tuf stopped adjusting his chaps and stood with his hand over his heart as the words to "The Star-Spangled Banner" rang out. Someone called his name but he didn't move nor did he plan to. In his mind's eye he could see Corporal Charles Hoffman lying with a hole in his chest, blood gushing out.

"Tuf Hart!"

Tuf pulled the marine's body behind a rock to safety. "Everything will be okay," he promised. But it wasn't.

Charles closed his eyes and died in Tuf's arms. Nothing would ever be okay again.

The song ended and Tuf turned to the man calling him.

"Hey, didn't you hear me?" a man with a clipboard asked.

Tuf poked a finger hard into the man's chest. "Didn't you hear the national anthem being sung?"

"Huh?"

"The national anthem. Don't you have enough respect to stop for a moment to honor the men and women who died for your freedom?"

The man drew back with a scowl. "You talk as if you were in the service."

"I was. Marines. Staff Sergeant Tomas Hart."

The man's ruddy complexion turned a funny shade of white. "Look, man, I'm just trying to find Tuf Hart."

"That's me."

"Oh. I…I just wanted to tell you you'll be the fifth rider and the horse you drew is Teddy Bear."

"I already know that."

"Just making sure so everything will run smoothly. Bareback riding should start in about five minutes." The man walked away.

Colt strolled over. "Lighten up. You scared him to death."

"I wanted to drive my fist through his face."

Colt shook his head.

"I'm sorry. I lost it for a moment." He bent to finish strapping on his chaps, trying to blend reality with the horror of war.

"Tuf…"

"Don't worry," he told his brother. "I'm not a violent person. The man's disrespect just got to me."

"If you want to talk, I'm here."

"I know, and thanks, but I'm fine." He exhaled a harsh breath and tried to push the incident out of his mind. "Let's rodeo."

Jesse Hobbs was up first on Powder Puff. He made the ride and scored a 79. Trey Watson was next with a 79.5 ride. Bossy Lady charged into the chute, and Colt climbed the steel rail to help Cory Kinney prepare to ride. The horse bucked wild, but Cory managed to stay on and scored an 80.

Beau took over the job of helping the cowboys. The next rider bit the dust, too, on a horse named Dixie Chick. Then it was Tuf's turn. Teddy Bear was in the chute. Tuf donned his protective vest and climbed the steel rail. At the top, he blocked the crowd, the sounds and the scents from his mind. The horse fidgeted, not liking the chute.

"Stay focused," Beau advised.

Tuf slid onto the horse and checked his rigging. It was cinched tight around the horse's withers. Tuf slipped his gloved hand into the handle and gripped with all his strength. He got his legs into position, leaned slightly back and raised his left hand. Ready, he nodded and the gate flew open. When the horse's front hooves hit the ground, Tuf marked the horse at the shoulders with his spurs. Before he could get a rhythm marking, the horse gave a wild buck, and he found himself lying flat on his face in the dirt.

"Damn!" He got to his feet, dusted off his new chaps and picked up his hat.

The rest of the rodeo he helped with the Hart stock, getting them in chutes and out. Colt made his ride, as did Beau. They'd probably place in the money if they made their ride tomorrow night.

They were dog-tired by the time they made it to the trailer for the night.

"Who gets the bed?" Beau asked, removing his dirty shirt.

"Since it's my trailer, I get half the bed." Colt made his opinion known.

"That's cool," Beau said. "I'll sleep on the kitchen-table converter bed. I'll be talking to Sierra before I go to sleep and that way I won't disturb anyone."

A knock sounded at the door. Tuf looked at Colt and Beau. "Expecting anyone?" They shook their heads. Tuf turned the latch to find two girls standing there, one blonde and the other brunette, in tight jeans and even tighter blouses. They wore cuffs like he'd seen Cheyenne make on their wrists.

"Is Colt Hart here?" the blonde asked.

"Uh..." He glanced over his shoulder to see Colt waving his arms above his head and mouthing *no.* "Uh...he's unavailable."

"That's a pity. We're going to a party and Colt loves parties."

"He's married now."

The girl cocked an eyebrow. "Married? When did that happen?"

Tuf didn't know the exact date, and before he could reply, Colt walked up. "Hi, Cindy, Mallory."

"Colt," the girls screeched in unison.

Colt shoved his hands into his jeans. "Sorry, I'm a family man now. Got kids and everything."

"Oh, we hadn't heard." The blonde made a face. "Such a shame. We could have had a great time."

"Hope you enjoy the rodeo." Colt backed into the trailer like an inchworm.

Cindy batted her eyes and looked Tuf up and down. "How about you, cowboy? Would you like to go to a killer party?"

"Uh…no, but thanks."

"Why doesn't anyone want to have fun anymore?" Cindy mumbled.

"Uh…night." Tuf closed the door and looked at his brother. "I'm proud of you."

Colt shrugged. "Figured it was time to stop hiding and be an adult."

"You know, Colt," Beau said from his perch at the kitchen table, "you should have some flyers printed up announcing your marriage so all the girls on the rodeo circuit will know, because clearly some haven't heard the news."

Colt raised his hand but restrained himself from shooting Beau the finger. Instead he headed for the bedroom. "Think I'll call my wife and tell her what a catch she's landed."

Tuf sank into the booth at the table. "Yeah, that's going to go over big." Colt laughed as he closed the small door. Tuf glanced at Beau. "Want to flip a coin to see who gets the shower first?"

"Nah. You go first. I'm waiting for a call from Sierra."

After his shower, Tuf pulled on jeans, a T-shirt and a jacket. Colt and Beau were each on the phone with their wives. He slipped out the door and sat on the trailer step. The night was chilly but not uncomfortable. He wrinkled his nose. Since the stock pens were a short distance away, the scent of alfalfa and manure wafted on the breeze.

Sticking his hand into the pocket of his jacket, he found his cell and clicked Cheyenne in his address book. She answered immediately.

"Hi, Tuf. How did you do?"

He grimaced. "I got bucked off."

"You'll do better. I know you will."

Her warm voice was soothing. "I hope it's not too late to call."

"No. The girls are out for the night and I'm making jewelry."

He settled against the trailer door. "Did they ride today?"

She laughed softly and it eased every ache in him. "I could hardly keep them focused on their lessons today. They wanted to ride instead. Guess why it was so important?"

"Why?"

"So they can show Tuf how good they can ride all by themselves."

Tuf grinned up at the twinkling stars.

"I made a short video with my cell. I'll send it to you."

"Okay." He clicked off and waited for the beep. Then he opened the video. Astride the horses, dressed in matching pink and purple outfits, including hats and boots, Sadie and Sammie waved excitedly at him. He could hear their voices.

"Hi, Tuf," Sadie said. "We can ride real good."

"I was 'posed to say that," Sammie complained.

"No, I was," Sadie corrected her.

"I was," Sammie insisted.

"Girls." Cheyenne's voice rang out. "Do you have anything to say to Tuf? Sammie first."

"She's a big baby," Sadie grumbled.

"Am not."

"Sammie, say something quick." Mother director was on the job.

"I love you, Tuf."

"I love you, too, Tuf." Sadie wasn't going to be outdone.

"I love you, too," he murmured as the screen went black. Holding the phone in his hand, he wondered how that could have happened so quickly. They'd stolen his heart, much as their mother had years ago. His cell buzzed and he clicked on.

"I forgot to tell you they weren't on their best behavior."

"I thought they were cute."

"You would."

There was a long pause, and he could feel her doubts seeping through.

"Tuf…we agreed to be friends, but things are changing too fast. My girls are becoming attached to you and…"

"What?"

"I don't want them to get hurt."

His hand gripped the phone. "You think I'd hurt them?"

"Not intentionally, but you're a former marine and you've been through a great deal. I couldn't help Ryan and…"

"Cheyenne…" The only thing he could do was be honest. "Yes, I came back scarred, but I had a counselor at the hospital in Maryland and I see one in Billings. I've done everything I can to heal."

"Oh, Tuf."

He held the phone a little closer to his ear. "If I thought for one minute I could harm you or the girls, I'd walk away now."

"I…I don't want you to walk away."

"Good." He relaxed. "Then let's go on a date, the four of us."

She laughed, a tingly sound that seemed to light up the night.

"And don't you dare say no."

"Yes, Tuf Hart, I will go out with you."

He never realized until that moment that he'd been waiting ten years for her to say that.

Chapter Ten

The darkness of the trailer threw him as he slipped back in. A tiny light burned in the kitchen area. Beau slept on the makeshift table bed and Colt was out in the bedroom. Had he and Cheyenne been talking that long? Yanking off his jacket and jeans, he crawled over Colt and snuggled under the blanket. Colt didn't even stir. He always slept like a log.

As sleep claimed him, he heard her words, *"Yes, Tuf Hart, I will go out with you."* That would sustain him for a while.

Some time toward dawn when his defenses were down and he was weak, bad memories snuck through like thieves stealing his well-earned peace of mind. He was back on that hill in Afghanistan where Michael had been shot, bullets blasting all around him. Frank Bigby screamed and went down. Tuf and another marine dragged Frank behind a rock, out of the line of fire.

"I'm hit, Tomas. It hurts."

"I know. Take a deep breath. Stay here. We'll pick you up on the way down."

"Tomas…"

"You're fine. It's just a shoulder wound."

Mortar fire exploded above them. "Stay down. Stay down!" he shouted to his men. When there was a lull, he jumped to his feet. "Let's go. Let's go!" They charged forward, avoided enemy fire when they could. The Afghan soldier went down.

He had to stay focused. He'd check him once the battle was over. They were almost at the top. A few more feet and they could take out the enemy. "No, no, no!" He had to look. "No!"

"Tuf! Tuf! Tuf!"

Someone held him down. Had the enemy captured him? He had to fight. He had to get away.

"Tuf, damn it! Wake up!"

He opened his eyes and saw Colt sitting on top of him. Beau held his arms. "Oh, no!" They released him and he sat on the side of the bed, his head in his hands. Colt and Beau sat beside him.

"Do you want to talk?" Colt asked.

"No."

"You were screaming and thrashing about. I think you were back in Afghanistan."

Tuf jumped to his feet and grabbed his clothes. "I have to get out of here."

"Tuf."

Within a minute he was dressed and hit the door.

"Tuf!"

He ran until his lungs could no longer hold air and then he sank to the cold ground. The stock pens were in front of him. Midnight stared at him and suddenly the nightmare eased. He was home, away from the horror.

Brushing the nightmare from his mind, he got to his feet and walked over to Midnight. "Good morning, boy."

The horse pawed the ground and Tuf relaxed, but he still didn't understand why he was having the debilitating dream again. He hadn't had one in months. Something must have triggered it. A gush of air left his throat in realization—the man who wouldn't pause for the national anthem. That had to be it.

Slowly, he made his way back to the trailer, feeling trapped in a war he couldn't escape. Last night he'd been so happy, but now he couldn't see any kind of relationship with Cheyenne. She'd had one marine who'd suffered from PTSD. He couldn't do that to her again.

When he entered the trailer, Colt and Beau were at the table eating breakfast tacos and drinking coffee. No one said anything and he sat down next to Beau. Colt slid a taco and a cup of coffee toward him. He wrapped his hands around the warm cup and took a swallow. Then he undid the tin foil around the egg-and-sausage taco and ate it. Still no one spoke.

Tuf set his cup on the table. "Somebody say something. Please."

Colt shrugged. "We don't know what to say."

"Just don't look at me like that."

"Like what?"

"With pity."

Colt sighed. "Tuf, I can't even imagine what you've been through, but last night Beau and I got an up-close-and-personal view of something horrific. We're not looking at you with pity. We're looking at you in awe."

"Yeah," Beau agreed. "Do you want to talk?"

He shook his head. "I've talked to a counselor about my experiences until I'm blue in the face. I guess some of those memories are always going to be with me." He wadded the tin foil into a ball. "Could we talk about something else now?"

"Sure." Colt settled back. "Last night after I finished talking with Leah, I took a shower and noticed you weren't in the trailer. I looked outside and saw you on the step talking on your cell. Who were you talking to?"

"Cheyenne," he admitted.

"Ah." Colt nodded. "Leah mentioned you came to the rescue of the infamous runaway Sadie."

"Yeah. Cheyenne and I are friends. We're just talking."

Beau punched his shoulder. "Well, that's a lot more than you did in high school."

"You had a big crush on her back then," Colt added.

He frowned. "Did everybody in Roundup know that?"

"Everybody but Cheyenne." Colt pushed away from the table. "We have to get to work. We have a rodeo tonight."

"Let's go," Tuf said and paused briefly as a tiny remnant of the dream lingered. He pushed it away and hoped it was gone for a long, long time.

The rest of the day went smoothly. They had two jobs: getting the animals into the chute to ride and supporting each other and the cowboys. Then they had to make sure the animals made it back to the stock pen without injury. After a ride, an animal was usually hyper, hard to settle down. But there were several handlers to help. They trusted no one with Midnight, though. Ace would be proud of the way Colt took care of the horse that the future of Thunder Ranch rode on.

The spotlights came on and people filed into their seats, chattering. Noise erupted around the arena. "Should've Been a Cowboy" by Toby Keith blared over the speakers. In the cowboy-ready area, it was a whole different scene. The chutes banged while cowboys worked on their gear, psyching themselves up for a good ride. Tuf was no different. As he tightened the straps on his spurs, the announcer asked for everyone to stand for the national anthem. Standing, he once again placed his hand over his heart and remembered his buddies and other soldiers who had died in the line of duty for their country.

When the music ended, he turned to see the man with the clipboard. Tuf nodded and squatted to finish adjusting his spurs.

"Mr. Hart, I…um…"

Tuf rose to his feet and stared at the man, realizing for the first time that he was probably about twenty years old.

"I…I'm sorry about last night. I have a cousin in the navy and I would never disrespect our military. Working the rodeo is a dream job for me. I got so busy with details, I wasn't paying attention. I won't make that mistake again."

"I appreciate that."

The kid glanced at the clipboard. "You're second up tonight on True Grit. You got about five minutes."

"Thank you." Tuf held out his hand and the kid shook it vigorously.

"Thank you, sir," he said and walked off.

Colt hurried over. "Did you get into it again with him?"

"No. He apologized."

"That's good." Colt looked him up and down. "You ready?"

"Yep." They strolled to the chutes and watched as Jesse Hobbs slid onto Naughty Girl. The horse burst from the chute and bucked one way, and Jesse went in the opposite direction, landing on his stomach.

True Grit waited in the next chute. Tuf anchored his hat and climbed the chute. The horse was restless, moving about. Carefully, he slid on, balancing himself on the cold steel of the chute. True Grit jerked his head, not liking the baggage. Tuf tested his rigging and stuck his right hand into the handle.

"Stay focused," Colt suggested. "This horse is not known for consistency. Be prepared for anything."

"Got it." He placed his legs into position and raised his left arm. When he nodded, the side of the chute opened, and True Grit leaped out and bucked into the arena. Tuf held his feet in position over the break of the horse's shoulders until the horse's front feet hit the ground. He marked the horse, and while maintaining control, he moved his boots in a toes-turned-out, rhythmic motion in tune with the horse's bucking motion.

Three seconds. Four seconds. His muscles stretched, and he felt like his arm was being pulled out of its socket, but he kept marking the horse with his spurs. Eight seconds. The buzzer sounded, and he leaped from the bucking bronc and landed on his feet. Yes! He'd made the ride. Walking toward the chute, he watched for his score on the board. Seventy-eight. Not bad.

He swung over the arena fence and made his way to the cowboy-ready area. Removing his chaps and spurs, he placed them in his bag. Beau would take his rigging off True Grit. He hurried to help Colt, and he wanted to be there when Midnight made his appearance. Cory Kinney had drawn Midnight and he was scheduled to go last.

Tuf remembered Cory. He'd made it to the national finals last year and had placed sixth overall. He was an up-and-coming bareback rider, and Tuf wondered how he'd do on Midnight.

"Great ride," Colt said as Tuf climbed the chute. Trey Watson was about to ride. "Take over. I have to get Midnight ready."

They watched as Trey scored a seventy-nine, putting him ahead of Tuf. That was okay because Tuf knew he wasn't going to win tonight. His no-ride last night had put him out of the money.

Midnight shot up the alley leading to a chute. Tuf quickly opened the gate and slammed it shut behind the black horse. Colt was already on the chute getting Midnight geared up to ride. Tuf didn't get too close because his presence always seemed to rile the horse, as if he knew they were adversaries and would one day challenge each other.

Once Midnight was reasonably calm, Colt motioned to Cory, who climbed the chute. Colt attached the flank strap lined with fleece, and Midnight jerked his head up. Carefully, Cory climbed on. Midnight's body trembled with restless energy. Several minutes passed as Cory adjusted his rigging. Once he gave the signal, the chute opened, and Midnight reared up on his hind legs and leaped forward, kicking out with his powerful back legs. One strong kick and Cory flipped over backward, landing near the chute. Midnight ran wild in the arena and the crowd roared.

"Damn, what a ride," Colt said.

"I think you mean a no-ride," Tuf corrected him.

"I better get Midnight settled down before it's my time to ride."

Tuf continued to take care of the animals in the chute. Colt had a good saddle-bronc ride and he'd place in the money. When barrel racers came on, Tuf watched for a moment and remembered Cheyenne. He'd been forcing himself not to think of her, but suddenly he could see her racing into the arena on Jewel and flying around the barrels in graceful movements. No one rode a horse like Cheyenne. He took a deep breath and forced those thoughts away. They would haunt him later, though.

It was almost midnight when they made their way to the trailer. They were bone-tired, but Colt and Beau had a spring in their steps because they'd earned some money for Thunder Ranch. His brother and cousin were talking to their wives so he took a quick shower and crawled into bed. He paused for a moment and thought of calling Cheyenne, but it was late and he wasn't sure what to say to her now.

Was he always going to be trapped in that war?

TUF LAY STARING INTO the semidarkness. Colt and Beau were in the kitchen area, still talking to their wives. The light from the sink spilled across the bed, but it didn't bother him. He welcomed it. If he closed his eyes and fell asleep, he was afraid the nightmare would return. The only way to ward it off was to stay awake. And that was crazy. His counselor had said he had something deep-seated in him that he didn't want to face. He'd gone over every horrible moment of his stint in the marines, and he still didn't know what it was.

He flipped onto his side, intending to stay awake as long as he could. He didn't want to subject Colt and Beau to a repeat of last night. And he never wanted Cheyenne to see a glimpse of his hell. What were his options? Not many. He'd have to stop seeing her. A new kind of pain twisted his gut. Everything he'd ever wanted was just out of his reach.

THE NEXT MORNING THEY were up early to load their stock and make the long trip home. Tuf's plan of staying awake hadn't worked. He'd been too tired. The next thing he knew, dawn had arrived, peeping in at a new day. After a quick breakfast, they loaded the stock and prepared to leave Bozeman. They stopped for gas and then rolled onto the U.S. 191 and headed for home.

After almost four hours, they turned the trucks onto Thunder Road. Tuf parked the Airstream in its spot, and Colt backed the cattle carrier to the chute. Once Midnight was unloaded and in his paddock, Colt turned to Tuf.

"Can you handle it? I want to see Leah."

"Go." He waved a hand. "You, too, Beau. I got it."

He didn't have to tell them twice. Colt grabbed the zipped leather bag with the money and paperwork and dashed to the office to leave it in the safe. A few minutes later, Tuf saw him sprinting across the yard to his double-wide. Beau had disappeared faster than he could blink. Evidently, the honeymoon wasn't over.

After unloading, he parked the cattle carrier in its spot. He then fed the animals and made his way to the house.

He heard voices in the backyard and went there. His mom sat in a redwood recliner, watching Jill and Davey playing in the yard with a ball.

"Tomas, you're back." His mom smiled.

He kissed her forehead and sat in a chair beside her.

She turned to face him. "I saw Cheyenne and her girls in church this morning."

His stomach tightened.

"When Cheyenne told them I was your mother, well, one of them, I can't tell them apart, was Tuf this and Tuf that. Soon the other twin joined in. They're waiting for you to come home to show you how good they're riding." She lifted an eyebrow. "Shouldn't you be over there?"

Clasping his hands between his knees, he didn't respond.

He could feel his mom's eyes on him. "Tomas, do not disappoint those little girls."

He stood to make a quick getaway.

"Tomas Hart." She stopped him in his tracks. "What's wrong with you?"

He took a deep breath. "I have a lot to sort out. I'll talk to you later."

"Tomas…"

He didn't turn back. He was running—running scared. *Coward* echoed through his mind. He never thought of himself as a coward. Placing his hand over his left jeans pocket, he traced the shape of the Silver Star. He wasn't a coward.

But he sure felt like one.

Chapter Eleven

Cheyenne kept glancing at her watch. Almost five. Why hadn't Tuf called or come by? She'd been waiting since she'd seen the cattle carrier and Airstream trailer go by. And the girls kept asking when Tuf was coming. She'd run out of things to tell them. "He's working and has a lot to do" was beginning to sound flimsy. The girls were sitting on the front porch in their boots, jeans and cowgirl hats. What if Tuf didn't come? What was she going to tell them then?

Feeling anxious, she put down the necklace she was working on. She was making a mess of it. The turquoise stones were expensive and deserved her full attention. She placed them in a tray and stored them in her workbox. She'd finish it later.

Tucking her hair behind her ears, she took a long breath. It hadn't been easy to open her heart again. And to another marine, at that, but she felt a connection to Tuf. It was real, as real as anything she'd ever felt. He was kind, patient, understanding and cared about her girls. That was real, too. Before she'd known it, she was taking steps toward him instead of away like her mind had dictated. She'd been burned badly, so why was she exposing her emotions once again to the fire?

She gathered her jewelry-making supplies and took them to her room. They'd had a wonderful conversation on Friday night so she didn't understand his silence today. Something had to have happened. But what? She was tired of trying to figure it out. She'd take the girls to get ice cream or a hamburger or both to get their minds off Tuf. As she placed her box in an old armoire in her room, she heard the girls screech.

They must have spotted a bug. She ran to the front door, preparing to be the bug slayer, but stopped short in the doorway. Tuf stood there with Sadie in one arm and Sammie in the other. *He's here.* Her heart thumped against her ribs in excitement. She grabbed her jacket, slipped into it and stepped outside.

The girls chattered away. When they saw Cheyenne, they squirmed to be let down. Sadie asked, "Mommy, how long is five minutes?"

She understood the question. How long to tell Tuf to wait before coming to the barn to watch them ride. They wanted to get ready.

"Oh, a long time."

"Good." Sadie looked up at Tuf. "Five minutes and then come watch us."

"You got it, munchkin."

Sadie took Sammie's hand and walked down the steps and headed for the barn. Cheyenne reached for her cell in her pocket and called her dad. "The girls are almost there." She clicked off and stared into Tuf's dark eyes. He looked tired…and sad. Something had happened.

"Could we talk for a minute?" he asked.

"Sure." He sat on the step and she sat beside him, preparing herself for his next words.

He clasped his hands between his knees. "I could have

come over earlier but…I think it's best if I don't see you anymore."

Her stomach cramped with an old, familiar pain. Ryan had never given her a chance to help him. He'd always pushed her away.

She faced him and wavered at the pain she saw there. "What happened? Just tell me."

He looked at his clasped hands and he seemed to grip them tighter. "I haven't had a nightmare in six months and I thought I was past that, but while in Bozeman, I had a bad one. Colt said I was screaming and thrashing about. He and Beau were holding me down when I woke up."

Unable to stop herself, she placed her hand on the arm beneath his denim jacket. His muscles were rigid, tight. "I'm sorry."

"I don't want you to see me like that. You went through hell with Ryan."

He was trying to protect her, and for a moment she couldn't speak. Ryan never opened up like this or ever gave her a chance to help him. Tuf was different. She sensed it.

"Did you hit Colt or Beau?"

"What?" He blinked in confusion. "I don't think I did. They didn't say. I just wanted to run until I couldn't feel that pain anymore."

"Ryan was the opposite. He'd become violent, throwing and breaking things. When I would try to calm him, he'd hit me and then leave the house and go to a bar and drink. The next day he'd apologize, but it happened over and over again. I stayed because I knew he couldn't control what was happening to him, but as the girls got older, I knew I'd have to go because he was starting to get angry at them." She took a burning breath. "I don't think you're like that. I've known you all my life and I've never seen you do a violent thing, except ride bucking horses."

"Cheyenne…"

She heard the entreaty in his voice. "What's really bothering you?"

He looked down at her hand still on his sleeve. "I don't want to hurt you in any way. And I'm afraid I will."

"Tuf…"

"You've been through enough."

So have you.

His inner turmoil was a tangible thing. He was trying hard to live again, but the war kept pulling him back. She ached to help him. How? She couldn't help Ryan, so how could she help him? A sense of inadequacy swept over her.

He got to his feet. "I'll take a rain check on our date."

She stood, too, and a chill ran through her. Wrapping her arms around her waist, she said, "Maybe that's best."

Without another word, he swung toward his truck.

"Tuf."

He turned around.

"The girls are waiting for you. Please don't disappoint them."

They made their way to the barn, and the girls happily showed off on their horses. Her dad had spray painted the barrels bright yellow, and they slowly made the figure eight around them. Afterward, Tuf walked away to his truck.

This time, she knew he wouldn't be coming back.

THE NEXT DAY AFTER HIS RUN, Tuf quickly showered and changed into jeans and a Western shirt. He hadn't stopped at the Wright house. Not that he didn't want to. It would only hurt her more. Snapping the light blue chambray, he paused. Cheyenne had helped picked out the shirt. Maybe then they'd both known their lives would reconnect. The odds were against them, though. He was a mess. She was a mess. And there didn't seem to be a way around all the baggage they carried. It was best to end it now before their hearts were involved. He wasn't so sure that his wasn't already fully committed.

Strolling across the yard, he noticed Ace's, Colt's, Beau's, Duke's and Uncle Josh's trucks parked at his mom's office. It wasn't even seven yet. Something was up.

As he walked in, Colt said, "Finally, Tuf's here. We can start the meeting?"

His mom sat at her desk with Uncle Josh on her right and Ace on her left. The others were standing around the coffee machine.

Tuf made a face at his brother. "I wouldn't have run if I'd known y'all were going to be here this early."

"Hmm." Duke gave a lopsided grin. "I saw you outside Cheyenne Sundell's driveway."

He hadn't even noticed the headlights. He must have been really distracted. "I just stopped for a second." It was one of those moments he didn't want to admit to. He wanted to see her, but knew it was best if he just kept running.

"You seeing Cheyenne this early in the morning?" Colt asked with a mischievous glint in his eyes.

"Stop teasing your brother," his mother broke in. "He has a lot more muscle now, and I'm too old to be breaking up fights."

"Ah, Mom, we don't fight anymore," Colt told her. "We just bait each other. Ace is best at it. He uses a verbal cattle prod to keep us in line."

"Someone has to," Ace said out of the corner of his mouth.

"See." Colt pointed a finger at his brother, laughing.

Their mother gave them a look that was as quelling as any words she could have spoken. The room became quiet and they pulled up folding chairs to sit around the desk.

Sarah slipped on her reading glasses and shuffled through the papers in front of her.

"I spoke with Dinah and she said whatever we decide is fine with her. She has her hands full with the sheriff's job and her pregnancy." She laid her glasses on top of the papers. "Leah and I have gone over the books, and we're still not making ends meet. The economy is killing us. The price of feed and gas continues to rise. We have a balloon payment coming due on our note June first, and we're ten thousand short even with the money Tomas deposited into the ranch account. That's the bottom line. I really thought we could make a success of the contracting business, but all our problems with Midnight have sorely hurt us."

She leaned back in her chair, and Tuf thought how worried and tired she looked. "I'm not sure what to do now. I've thought about this for days, and the only option I see is to sell the three thousand acres we lease and all our cattle and rodeo stock. We could pay off the note, and everyone could start over with decent nine-to-five jobs. And, Ace, your vet business would be safe and unencumbered by ranch debt."

Stunned silence filled the room. No one knew what to say or do. Sarah Hart wasn't a quitter, but it felt as if she held a grenade in her hand and was about to pull the pin to end all their dreams.

Colt leaped to his feet. "Hell, no. I've worked too hard for too long for it to end like this."

"Aunt Sarah," Beau spoke up, "Tuf and I are set to rodeo, and Colt will be catching every rodeo close to home. If we can't earn ten thousand by June, then we're not fit to be called cowboys."

Duke got to his feet. "Aunt Sarah, I'll continue to help transport stock in my off time and help all I can around here."

"Sarah." Uncle Josh put his arm around his sister. "What's going on with you? I want to spend more time with Jordan, but I don't plan to abandon my duties to Thunder Ranch."

"Yeah, Mom, are you not feeling well?" Ace looked closely at their mother.

"I feel fine." She glanced at family photos hanging on the wall. "I'm just feeling a little melancholy." Her eyes swung to a family picture on her desk. "None of you know what day it is, do you?"

That only confused them further.

"It's John's and my fortieth wedding anniversary. We were so young when we got married and money was tight. Land was cheap back then and we saved to buy our own place. Every extra dollar went to buy more land. We lived in a small trailer and survived on beans and rice. It was a struggle but we did it. Cattle prices were good and we started to make money. When I became pregnant, we decided to build the house we wanted. We brought Aidan home to the new house." She paused for a second. "I can't help thinking that I'm back where I started—struggling. I want better for my kids and nephews, so I decided to give you boys a choice. That's what this is about."

Tuf rose to his feet. "No choice, Mom. We're the Harts and the Adams, and we're not looking for a way out. We're in this for the long haul. I know I didn't do too good in Bozeman, but like Dad used to say, 'You get bucked off, you pick yourself up and do better next time.' That's what I plan to do, so stop worrying. If worse comes to worst, I'll sell my truck. But I don't think I'll have to do that. As you know, Midnight did very well at the rodeo."

"That's a small thing, son. The horse could get hurt as he has before."

"Have you seen how Colt takes care of that horse? He

treats it like one of his kids. And Cory Kinney, an experienced cowboy who made it to nationals last year, couldn't stay on after the first buck. That's going to spread around the circuit, and cowboys are going to want to test their skill on the horse. Midnight will gain attention, and Thunder Ranch will gain more rodeo contracts and breeding fees. It's not the ending, Mom. It's the beginning."

"I agree with Tuf." Ace stood. "I know I was worried about Midnight being injured, but Colt has proven he can control the horse. I don't think there's a need for a vote. You know how we all feel, but you have the right to outvote us. What's it going to be?"

For the first time, a smile spread across his mom's face. "I say I got the answer I really wanted. You boys have turned into fine young men and I'm proud of you." She got to her feet. "Flynn is helping Aidan today and I'm playing Grandma." The worry in her blue eyes vanished.

Uncle Josh followed her to the door. "I'll bring Jordan over. She loves babies."

Ace moved to the computer. "We have to figure out what we have to do to ease Mom's mind."

"Let's check rodeo schedules and see where we can make the most money," Tuf suggested.

For the next thirty minutes, they debated rodeos. "Right now the best money is down south, mainly Texas," Colt said.

Ace pondered this. "Tuf and Beau, you can head south. Colt can rodeo here in Montana, South and North Dakota, and Wyoming. That's closer to home. How does that sound?"

"Like a plan," Colt said, "but my rodeo time is limited because of Midnight. The more we get him out there, the more his reputation is going to grow."

"Yeah, we have to consider that, too." Ace pondered some more. "When Midnight bucks, I want you there."

"I plan to be." Colt nodded.

"Okay. The goal is to make as much money as possible."

"We got it," Tuf said, and he and Beau spent time on the computer planning their schedule.

Later he helped with the broncs and the bulls. Then he checked on the cows. When he returned to the house, his mom was playing with Emma, smiling. She was so different than she was this morning. The worry had been lifted from her shoulders. He would make every rodeo he could to earn money to ease her mind. And to make up for all the years he wasn't here.

BEFORE TUF LEFT TO RODEO, he saw a counselor at the Veteran's Administration in Billings. He was never good at opening up about his feelings, but he knew if he wanted to be whole again he had to talk.

Since the counselor had his records from the navy hospital in Maryland, he was already aware of Tuf's story, so he tentatively began to tell the counselor about the recent nightmare, and about Cheyenne and the girls. He came away with mixed feelings. The man agreed with the counselor in Maryland—Tuf had something deep inside him that he didn't want to face. After an hour of sharing brutal war memories, it became clear that whatever was bothering him was buried so deep he might never be able to reveal the pain—even to himself.

But the doctor urged him to remember the good things going on in his life, especially his family and rodeoing. And he encouraged him to continue to talk to Cheyenne, but Tuf didn't know if that was possible. At least not until he got his head straight.

Chapter Twelve

The next morning he and Beau saddled up, so to speak, and headed out to hit the rodeo circuit. Tuf hugged his mom, said goodbye to his brothers and slid into the driver's seat.

As they passed the Wright property, he noticed the kitchen light was on. Cheyenne was making jewelry in her green robe and bright slippers. In his mind's eye, her beautiful features and intense concentration were clear, as were the tiny freckles across her cheekbones and nose.

"Why are you slowing down?" Beau asked.

"What?"

"If you want to stop and see Cheyenne, that's okay."

"No. We're just friends."

"Really?"

"Yep."

"From your expression I'm guessing you wish it was a lot more."

"Right now I'm focusing on rodeoing." It wasn't a lie—just not the exact truth.

"If you say so, coz." Beau pulled his hat over his eyes and went to sleep.

After a hundred miles, they switched drivers. Beau sang with the country tunes blaring from the radio. Tuf closed his eyes and tried to sleep, but he kept seeing Cheyenne's face.

On the way to Jackson, Mississippi, for the Dixie National Rodeo, they stopped for small-town rodeos in Wyoming, Colorado, Kansas and Oklahoma. It wasn't much money, but it helped to hone his skills and also helped to pay for food and motel bills. By the time they reached Jackson, he was ready.

The first night he was the sixth cowboy to ride. As always, Tuf had his equipment checked. The rowels had to be filed down so as not to hurt the horse. The stands were full and eager chatter resonated around the arena. Manure and rawhide were familiar scents. The bang of the chutes. The buzzer. It was rodeo time.

His muscles tensed before a ride. Donning his protective vest, he waited for the signal. Standing in the cowboy-ready area, three cowboys walked up to him. He recognized them: Cory Kinney, Jesse Hobbs and Trey Watson. They were dressed like Tuf, except each had their own signature chaps.

"Hey, didn't you ride in Bozeman?" Jesse asked.

"Yeah."

Jesse made the introductions.

"I'm Tuf Hart from Roundup, Montana." They shook hands.

"Wait a minute." Cory Kinney stepped forward. "Your family owns that black stallion."

"The Midnight Express."

"Cory's still talking about him." Trey laughed.

"That horse is powerful," Cory said. "Do you know where he'll buck next? I'd like another chance at him."

"I'll ask my brother." Tuf knew this would happen. News of Midnight was getting around. That was good for Thunder Ranch.

"This is my cousin Beau Adams," he said.

"Any kin to Duke Adams?" Cory asked.

"My brother," Beau replied.

"What happened to him? I don't see him on the circuit anymore."

"He got married." Beau shifted uneasily. Even though he'd come to grips about Duke's decision, there were times Tuf knew it still bothered him. But because of Beau's own marriage, he understood Duke's motivation a little better.

"Man, he let a woman mess with his head."

Before Beau could reply, Trey asked, "Where y'all headed next?"

"Texas."

"We are, too. Maybe we can buddy up and share expenses and fees."

"Fine by me." Tuf loved that about cowboys. They were always friendly and looking for ways to save money. But he worried about the sleeping arrangements and the nightmares.

"Great." Trey nodded. "I drive a 2003 Dodge and it's always breaking down. Probably because it has two hundred thousand miles on it. You drive anything better?"

"I have a decent truck."

The first rider was climbing the chute and they moved closer to watch. When it was Tuf's turn and he slid onto Black Widow, he heard the announcer. "Now we have a young cowboy from Roundup, Montana. He's a former marine and new to the circuit. Let's give a round of applause for Tuf Hart."

He worked his hand into the handle while Black Widow moved restlessly, eager to buck.

"How do they know that?" Tuf asked Beau, who was helping him with his rigging.

"Word gets around, I guess." Beau leaned away. "This

horse bucks wild. Be prepared for anything. Just maintain your rhythm."

It was a grueling week and the competition stiff. He finished third behind Cory and Trey and in the money. He was pleased. But it took a toll on his body as every muscle screamed for relief.

Later, they met the other cowboys and headed for Texas. There was a getting-to-know-each-other period. The cowboys teased Beau because he was a bull rider, and he took it all in good nature.

Every night Tuf worried he'd have the nightmare and scare the cowboys to death. But his luck was holding.

Their next stop was San Angelo, Texas, ten days of nonstop rodeoing. He and Cory were neck and neck through the whole event. Cory edged him out on the last night with an 88 ride. But Tuf still placed in the money, and he was able to send almost all of it home to his mom. He kept just enough for gas, food and lodging, which was much cheaper since his new friends were sharing the cost.

Next rodeo was Fort Mohave, Arizona, then Marshall, Goliad, Nacogdoches and Lubbock, Texas. By now the cowboys had bonded, and once they saw Beau ride, they had a healthy respect for bull riders.

Tuf and Cory were fierce competitors, both determined to win and with a little luck make it to the finals in Vegas. Trey was the ladies' man, and after a lot of rodeos, he didn't make it back to the room until three or four in the morning. Jesse was easygoing and rodeos were fun to him.

But the constant traveling was getting to them. At the end of March, Tuf decided they needed a short break. Beau was about as Sierra-homesick as he'd ever seen. They dropped the cowboys in Mississippi, and he and Beau headed for Montana. And home. The first thing Tuf thought of was Cheyenne. As hard as he tried not to think of her, she was always on his mind.

CLASS IN SESSION. THAT's what the sign said on the closed kitchen door. After breakfast, Cheyenne let the girls play for a bit, and then she dressed them and they went to school, which just happened to be the kitchen. Once class started, the girls knew they had lessons to do. Sometimes they got sidetracked and wanted to laugh and play, but Cheyenne was very strict. She wanted them to be ready for kindergarten in the fall.

"Write your numbers," she said to Sadie.

"I already know my numbers."

"Write them anyway and then we'll count." Sadie was very good with numbers and counting while Sammie excelled in reading and the alphabet. Sammie followed instructions easily while Sadie usually balked until Cheyenne had to make her. They looked alike but they definitely had different personalities.

Sadie laid down her pencil and crossed her arms across her tiny chest. "I'm not writing no more numbers."

They had this battle almost every day. Sadie seemed to have a need to test her, and Cheyenne's patience was wearing thin. "Go to your room and sit in the time-out chair. You will not get any gummy bears after lunch or ride Toughie today. Go." She pointed toward the girls' room.

Tears rolled from Sadie's eyes and sobs racked her body. At the sight, Cheyenne's resolve wavered but she remained firm. "Go."

Sadie crawled from her chair, her little body shaking, and then she did a quick turn and threw herself at Cheyenne. Sobbing, she blubbered, "I'm sorry. I'm sorry."

Cheyenne picked her up and held her. "You have to mind Mommy."

"'Kay."

"I finished my number," Sammie said.

"Good, baby, you get an extra gummy bear after lunch."

That immediately grabbed Sadie's attention, and she scurried back to her chair and finished her numbers. Sitting back, Sadie asked, "Mommy, when is Tuf coming to see us?"

She wasn't startled by the question because they asked it every day. "I don't know, baby. He's at a rodeo far from home."

"But why doesn't he come home to see us? He likes us."

That was the hard part. Trying to explain something she didn't understand herself. Tuf didn't want to expose them to his nightmares, and Cheyenne wasn't sure if she could live with another marine with PTSD.

She thought of him constantly, though, and she'd been reading about PTSD on the internet. Tuf needed caring and support and for someone to listen when he wanted to talk. It seemed Tuf had done all the right things, but he was still struggling. She wondered if she'd let go of their relationship too quickly because of her own fears. Could she help him? Did she want to help him?

"I miss Tuf," Sammie muttered.

So do I.

In a short amount of time, she and Tuf had formed a special connection, and she missed him. She missed his early-morning knocks, his cold hands and warm heart.

In the afternoon, her dad helped Austin at his store, so Cheyenne had the girls' lesson around the coffee table in the living room. They worked on the alphabet. The workbook had the alphabet listed, but several letters were missing and they had to fill in the blanks. Sammie breezed through hers.

Sadie paused. "Mommy, what comes after *G?*"

"Look at the picture below. It gives you a clue."

"It's a hat."

"Think about it and see if you can get the first letter of *hat.*"

Sammie whispered to her sister.

"Sammie," Cheyenne scolded.

"I got it. *H.*" Sadie beamed a big smile.

Cheyenne scooted to sit between them. She wanted Sadie to finish on her own.

Afterward, she gave them a choice. "What would you like to read today?"

"Brown Bear, Brown Bear," Sadie shouted.

"The Cat in the Hat," Sammie said.

"Go to your room and get the books."

They darted off, and she picked up their workbooks and pencils. After she stored everything away, her dad came in.

"Are you finished?" he asked.

"Yes. We're going to read, but we can do that in their room."

"I just came in for some water." He opened the refrigerator and pulled out bottled water. "Austin and I went over to the diner for a cup of coffee, and Beau called Sierra. He and Tuf are on their way home for a couple of days. Sierra was all excited."

She tucked a curl behind her ear. "Is there a reason you're telling me this?"

"No." He screwed the top off the bottle and took a swallow. "The girls keep asking about Tuf."

"Dad." She sighed. "Tuf and I agreed not to see each other anymore. He has flashbacks just like Ryan and it's hard for both of us."

"But you want to see him?"

"Dad..."

"I'm going to the barn to feed the horses and then I promised Austin to help unload supplies." He looked at her. "I can see you're unhappy. That's all I'm saying."

As he left, she thought about what he said. She did want to see Tuf—more than she ever thought possible. But there was so much heartache standing between them. Was there a chance for them?

THE LAZY SUN HUNG LOW in the west as Tuf drove into Roundup. He dropped Beau at the diner and continued on. The girls played on the porch as he passed the Wright house. He had to force himself not to stop.

When he reached home, he left his laundry in the utility room and walked through the kitchen to the great room. The TV was on, and his mom sat with her feet up watching an old rerun of *Bonanza.*

"Now, that's what I like to see."

"Tuf!" His mom jumped up. "You're back." She hugged him.

"Yeah, for a couple of days. How's everything?"

"You boys are working so hard. I couldn't be prouder. Oh." She reached for her cell on an end table. "I'll call Ace and Colt and…"

He held up his hand. "We can meet in the morning. Don't interrupt their family time."

"Okay. Have you eaten?"

"No, but don't fix anything. I'm not hungry. I'll grab a sandwich later." He trudged upstairs and fell across the bed. His muscles ached and he was tired…and lonely. Empty. Lost, even. There. He'd admitted it. How could he feel that way in a big, loving family? Sometimes he'd felt like that as a kid. Ace and Colt were close in age, and Beau and Duke were inseparable. Dinah had her girlfriends. He was always the odd one out.

Joining the marines hadn't helped that feeling. It had only intensified. Maybe he was one of those people who would always be alone. But…when he was with Cheyenne, those feelings weren't there. He felt alive and full of dreams—for the two of them. And the munchkins. He slowly drifted into sleep

When he awoke, it was dark outside. After a shower, he walked over to the window and stared toward the Wright property. He wanted to talk to her so bad he hurt.

His cell buzzed and he hurriedly picked it up from the dresser. *Cheyenne.* He blinked, not sure he'd read the name right. It was her. He answered.

"Tuf, it's Cheyenne."

"Yes, I know." God, he'd know that voice anywhere. He heard it in his dreams.

"I heard you're back."

"Yeah. We leave again on Friday."

"Could we talk, please?"

"Cheyenne…" As much as he wanted to, he hesitated.

"I'd like to talk. That's all."

"I'll be right over." He couldn't keep resisting. But he wondered what they could talk about that wouldn't hurt both of them.

Chapter Thirteen

Cheyenne put down her phone and a shiver ran through her. She'd done it. She'd made a choice and followed her heart. Instinctively she knew they had something special, and she was willing to work on their relationship. But was he?

She applied a touch of lipstick and headed for the front porch. The girls were asleep and her dad was helping Austin unload supplies for the store.

In minutes he pulled into her driveway. He slid out of the truck and his long, lean legs strolled toward her. The porch light showed off his handsome face and muscled body. Sexy. Brooding. That worked. A flutter of excitement rippled through her lower abdomen.

Without a word, he sank down by her on the step.

"How are you?" she asked before her nerves got the best of her.

"A little tired," he replied and looked at her.

She melted into his tortured gaze. He was hurting. That was obvious. All her feminine instincts kicked in and she wanted to help him. Before one word could leave her mouth, his eyes dropped to the necklace around her neck.

"That's gorgeous. Did you make it?"

She glanced down at the stainless-steel chain with embedded crystals. "Yes. The cornflower-blue crystals are

Yogo sapphires. I made a necklace for a lady using the stone, and I liked it so much I ordered the smallest crystals they had. It was all I could afford. They're mined in Rock Creek, Montana."

"They're almost as beautiful as your eyes."

She lifted an eyebrow. "My eyes are green."

"And brighter than any jewel."

She squinted at him. "You are tired."

"Mmm." He drew up his knees and rested his forearms on them. "What did you want to talk about?"

"Us," she answered without hesitation. "I've been doing a lot of thinking and reading about PTSD on the internet."

He turned his head, his eyes wide, but he didn't speak.

She rushed into speech before her brain could shut her up. "We've both admitted that we're attracted to each other and that we're afraid. I let fear control my reaction that day you said we shouldn't see each other anymore. I never wanted to get involved with another marine, especially one suffering from PTSD. But it's different with you and me. We've known each other all our lives, and I know in here—" she placed her hand over her heart "—that you would never intentionally hurt me. Do you think you can trust me not to fall apart when you have a nightmare? Do you think we can see each other again?"

She waited, her nerves stretched taut.

"The counselor said I have something deep inside me that I don't want to face. I feel it's something bad."

Scooting closer, she placed her hand on his tense arm. "Tuf Hart, I don't believe for one minute that you could do anything bad. No one would go back for that marine like you did. And help the man for two years? No one."

"Mmm."

Going on her own feminine intuition, she wrapped her arms around his waist and laid her head on his shoulder. Suddenly his arms cradled her gently against him. The moon engulfed them, and the stars twinkled with a delight that assured her she'd done the right thing. They needed each other.

She lifted her head and he bent his to steal a kiss. Except he didn't have to steal it. She gave freely, tasting the coolness that quickly turned heated and beyond her control. He kissed just as she knew he would—tenderly with a passion that promised pleasures beyond her wildest dreams.

His lips trailed a path to her forehead, and she sucked in air to cool her heated emotions.

"Are we more than friends now?" he asked.

"Definitely."

She stroked the stubble of his face and he caught her hand. "Are you sure, Cheyenne?"

"Yes. Just don't shut me out." She reached up and gently touched his lips. He drew her closer and they shared a long kiss.

They sat cuddled together. Out of the blue, he started talking about the war. "I wish I could remember what torments me in my sleep."

"Don't worry about it so much."

The big ol' moon stared at them and silently lit a path of dreams for lovers. And it was heavenly. A long time later, Tuf got in his truck and drove away.

She wrapped her arms around her waist, watching his taillights disappear out of the drive. But he would return. Oh, yeah!

THE NEXT MORNING TUF was up early, as usual. Last night there were no nightmares, just visions of Cheyenne's red hair splayed across his pillow. He was acting crazy and it felt good. For some time it had seemed as if a vise was clamped tight around his heart and he couldn't breathe or react in a normal way. It hurt too much.

He was finally free of the restriction. She didn't mind his nightmares. She had accepted him the way he was. He spent every minute of the day with Cheyenne and the girls. Cheyenne gave the twins a day off from school, and they rode their little hearts out for him, showing off. Sammie was a little daredevil at times. She was finally breaking out of her shell.

They had a late lunch at the diner, and the girls giggled and chatted like four-year-olds. Looking across the booth at Cheyenne, he saw his future. And it was normal and real. Something he'd thought he'd never have, but she was willing to take a chance on him. He was willing to meet her halfway and more.

All too soon it was time to leave. He held her, leaning against his truck. "We need time alone," he whispered against her lips.

"Next time you're home," she promised. "It will be X-rated."

After a long, heated kiss, Tuf drove away with that thought in his mind.

TUF AND BEAU HAD TO BE in Logandale, Nevada, for the Clark County Fair and Rodeo. From Nevada they headed to Corpus Christi, Texas, and then on to Old Settlers Reunion rodeo in Cheyenne, Oklahoma. The grueling schedule was taking its toll on them. Beau almost got trampled by a bull in Oklahoma and Tuf injured his shoulder, but he and Beau went on to the next rodeo. They ate junk food and sometimes slept in the truck. They both were feeling the strain of constant rodeoing. And eager to get home.

Dusk crept over the landscape as they rolled into Roundup. Tuf dropped Beau at the diner and sped home.

He talked to his mom, showered and changed clothes, and was on his way to Cheyenne's in record time.

His cell buzzed. Cheyenne. He'd talked to her about fifteen minutes ago. He hoped nothing was wrong.

"When are you leaving?" she asked.

"I'm on my way."

"I'll be waiting at the gate."

"Why?"

"If the girls see you, we won't be able to get away."

"Oh. Are they staying with Buddy?"

"Yes. They're gonna watch a movie. I'll explain later. Just hurry."

He zoomed down Thunder Road and his headlights caught her standing at the gate. She was beautiful in jeans, boots and a brown leather jacket. Her red hair was up and she was waving. He felt a kick to his heart. He couldn't believe how much he'd missed her. Before the truck came to a complete stop, he jumped out and wrapped his arms around her, pulling her tight against him. A delicate fragrance reached him and for a moment he just held her.

He ran his hands up her back beneath her jacket. "Oh, God, you feel so good."

She kissed his neck. "You feel pretty good, too."

Slightly turning his head, he caught her lips, and the coolness of the night vanished in the wake of heated emotions. She took his hand. "I have someplace much better in mind."

They crawled into the truck, and he couldn't resist stealing another kiss. "Where to, lady?"

"Billings."

"What?"

"I promised you a night alone, and I've booked a room at a hotel there."

He almost ran into the ditch, but he corrected quickly. "Are you sure?"

She cocked an eyebrow. "I am. How about you?"

"I'll see if I can make this thing fly."

She laughed that laugh that warmed his heart. On the way they talked about their lives. He'd talked to her every day, but it was much different in person. He could look at her, touch her.

"The girls are going to be so excited you're home."

"I can't wait to see them."

"You'll see a big difference. The horses and, of course, you got their minds on something besides their father. They never ask to go to his grave anymore. That worries me a little, but in other ways I feel it's good."

"It is." He reached out to touch her cheek, and she caught his hand and kissed it.

"They spent an afternoon with Dinah and Austin, and Dinah said they didn't ask for me once."

She gave directions, and he pulled into a hotel parking lot and found a spot. Hand in hand they went inside. The hotel was nice with large glass windows in the lobby decorated in a Western theme with Montana wildlife scenes and horse sculptures.

"Are we Mr. and Mrs. Jones?" he whispered in her ear.

She smiled. "Behave." The clerk at the counter gave her a key and they walked to the elevator. "The guy looked at me funny. I feel wicked."

In the elevator, he took her in his arms and kissed her. "I'm feeling rather wicked myself."

She stared at him with luminous eyes. "Don't tell me you haven't taken a girl to a hotel before."

"No. Well, not lately."

"Then we're leading very boring lives." She took his hand and led him down the red carpeted hall and stopped at their room number. "And that's about to change." She swiped the card across the door handle, and they went inside. The room was large with a king bed, sofa and a huge bath with a Jacuzzi. She glanced at her watch. "Home for the next two hours."

For the first time, he noticed she was nervous. A tiny vein in her neck pulsed wildly. He cupped her face. "You don't have to be nervous with me."

"It's just…"

"What?"

"After Ryan, I thought I would never have these feelings again."

"What feelings?" He found he was holding his breath.

She rested her head on his chest. "Overwhelming feelings. I think about you all the time, and it makes me do crazy things, like book a hotel room. But…but I feel that way because…because I love you. I probably have since high school."

His heart pounded so fast it seemed as if it sailed right through his chest into outer space. He lifted her chin so he could look into her eyes. "I love you, too. There's never been another girl for me."

"Oh, Tuf." She stepped back and let her jacket slide to the floor. Then she pressed herself against him. Every soft curve and angle sent his blood pressure soaring. He gently turned her and fell backward onto the bed. Her laughing green eyes stared down at him.

"Undo my shirt," he said huskily.

"That's easy." With one jerk, the snaps flew open, leaving his chest bare. She paused as she saw his bruised shoulder.

"I landed on it. It's fine."

"Tuf…"

"Shh. Kiss me." Her hands and lips touched his skin, and he groaned, quickly pulling her top over her head.

As their lips met, he thought this had to be the best night of his life.

A BUZZ WOKE CHEYENNE. Her cell alarm. She stirred against Tuf, loving the feel of his naked skin against hers. It was time to go, but it was hard to move with this heavenly lethargic feeling clinging to every muscle in her body.

She'd opened her heart to the most wonderful man, the way she should have ten years ago. She never thought she could love again. So much of her pride had been destroyed in her marriage. With Tuf it was different. She trusted him with her heart and her girls. She wasn't quite sure how that had happened so quickly, but Tuf's compassion for other people pulled her in like a big, hungry fish.

The most important factor was he was willing to talk about his PTSD. He wasn't shutting her out, and he listened to her stories about her defunct marriage without judging her. They'd found a way to connect, and it was oh, so great.

She lovingly stroked his dark hair from his forehead.

He opened one eye. "Did I hear a buzz? Or is that sound stuck in my head from so many rodeos?"

"I set my cell alarm. I want to get home by ten." She kissed his forehead, his nose. "That's Dad's bedtime and he won't go to bed unless I'm there, in case the girls wake up."

He hauled her into his arms and kissed her until she was limp with wanting. "Tuf…"

"I know." His lips trailed to the freckles across her cheekbones. "I couldn't resist."

They helped each other dress, and it was more titillating than it should have been. Finally, they were in the truck and they drove into her dad's driveway at five minutes to ten. The house was in darkness except for a lamp in the living room. Arm in arm they walked to the front door.

"Tonight was better than making an eight-second buzzer," he whispered against her lips.

She giggled. She couldn't help herself. "Tuf Hart."

"What? My whole life is defined by eight seconds."

"I hope it's not when we're making love."

"Oh, hell, no."

They laughed and held on a little while longer. "We have a family meeting in the morning to discuss finances, but I'll be here as soon as I can." He cradled her in his embrace. "Thanks for tonight."

"The start of many," she breathed into his neck.

"I better go, but I don't want to."

"Tomorrow," she said before he kissed her one last time and strolled to his truck.

Slowly, she went inside. Her dad was asleep in his chair, but he awoke the moment she opened the door.

"Have a good time?" He pushed to his feet.

"Wonderful. Are the girls asleep?"

"Like angels." He took a step toward the hallway and stopped. "You couldn't find a better man than Tuf Hart in the whole of Montana, and I'm glad you two are back together but, girl, take it slow. He's wounded on the inside and that takes time to heal. Just be careful."

"I will." She walked to the girls' room, straightened their covers and kissed them good-night, but all the while she was thinking about what her dad had said. Tuf *was* wounded on the inside, and she wasn't naive enough to think that love could heal that deep of a wound. But it could help to ease some of his pain.

As she crawled into bed, a niggling doubt persisted. Could their happiness be destroyed as easily as it had begun?

Chapter Fourteen

Tuf woke up full of energy. He hadn't felt this good in years. After dressing, he took the stairs two at a time. The only thing he wanted to do this morning was see Cheyenne. She fulfilled every one of his fantasies and then some. How was he supposed to think about rodeoing today?

In the kitchen, he poured a cup of coffee. His mother gave him a strange look.

"What?"

"You're in a good mood this morning."

"Why? Because I got a cup of coffee?"

"No. You're whistling."

"Oh." He hadn't even realized he was doing that.

"You must have had a good time last night with Cheyenne."

He straddled a chair. "We did."

"Eat your breakfast. We have to go to the office."

As they walked over, Tuf thought he'd give Ready a workout today. He tried to do that every time he was home, but now he just wanted to see Cheyenne.

Ace and Colt were already there. Beau and Uncle Josh strolled from Uncle Josh's house with a coffee cup in their hands. There was a round of good-mornings and his mom took her seat. After everyone had coffee, Sarah opened her ledger.

She shoved her glasses onto her nose. "Leah has all this on the computer, but I still like it on paper where I can see it. That's the way John and I did it for years, and it's hard to break old habits." She squinted at the open ledger. "You boys have been doing a wonderful job, but we're still short. I have no doubt, though, with the way Tomas and Beau are riding, that we'll make the note payment."

There was a round of high fives.

"But we've incurred more expenses. Josh and I purchased two one-year-old bulls out of the same line as Bushwhacker. They were a good price and I felt we shouldn't pass it up. Improving our stock with fresh blood is important. Also, we had to put new tires on the cattle carrier and gas prices have gone up once again, but I'm still optimistic. And Midnight is doing very well rodoeing thanks to Colt and his management of the horse. We get calls every day from cowboys wanting to know where he'll be bucking. They want a chance at the black stallion. I'm happy to say my instincts and Aidan's are paying off."

"Hot damn, I love good news." Colt grinned.

"But we have to keep doing what we're doing." His mom made that very clear.

"Don't worry, Mom," Ace said. "I think everyone realizes that."

"Yep." Tuf pulled up a chair. "Beau and I are making every PRCA-sanctioned rodeo we can. At the start of Cowboy Christmas in July, we'll make the big-money rodeos that count to build our points. With some luck, we'll make the big show in Vegas. If not, we'll still be earning money."

"Yeah," Beau added, "if I have to stay away from Sierra, I want to make it count for something."

"I appreciate what everyone is doing, but we have a long way to go."

Everyone knew that, and their focus was on one thing—saving Thunder Ranch.

CHEYENNE HAD A PLAN—to spend time alone with Tuf today.

She hurried around her bedroom, which was a chore in itself because it was cluttered. A trail led to the bed and a closet. Jewelry-making supplies occupied every other inch. Beads, stones, wire, spacers and tools littered her worktable pushed against one wall. Precious stones, jewels, supplies and expensive chains filled an armoire on the other wall. Next to it, boxes sat on the floor waiting to be mailed. On the far wall were her desk and computer. A dresser with her clothes was on the other side of the bed. The bed partially blocked a double window. Cramped and small, but it was all she had. What would Tuf think of all the clutter?

For a man who didn't care what color shirt he wore, he probably wouldn't even notice. That's why she loved him. He had a unique way of looking at the world. He didn't sweat the small stuff.

She brushed her hair and let it hang loose around her shoulders. Tossing the thick strands, she picked up a green flower clip she'd made and put it in her hair. Her freckles were naked just the way he liked them. As she applied lipstick, she heard a truck. She hurried to the front door.

Her attention was on Tuf getting out of his vehicle. Heavens, he was handsome and sexy with his long legs and muscled body. His Western shirt stretched across his broad shoulders and the Wrangler jeans were oh, so deliciously tight, fueling her imagination, which didn't need any fuel at all. He moved in a slow, easy stride, like a cowboy. She fanned herself and laughed at the same time. An aspirin might be required. She had it that bad.

Tuf bounded up the steps and gently pushed her inside, closing the door. His kiss was sweet, warm and intoxicating. Her head spun.

Between heated kisses, he asked, "Where's everyone?"

"Dad took the girls to buy more horse cookies from Angie and then they're going to the feed store to buy feed for the horses. After that, they're going for ice cream." She held up two fingers. "We have two hours."

He grinned and threw his hat onto the sofa. "I love a woman with a plan."

Tuf never noticed the clutter. His eyes were on her. Cupping her face, he slowly kissed her until she trembled with weakness. All thought left her. They discarded their clothes quickly and soon they were skin on skin, their hands and lips touching, caressing, stroking. She wasn't even aware of them moving to the bed, but she was very aware of his strong body, hot kisses and warm, erotic emotions shooting through her.

A long time later, they lay entwined and he stared into her eyes. "You're beautiful."

"So are you." She touched his bruised shoulder. "Does it hurt?"

"It's a little sore."

Caressing his shoulder, she suddenly stopped. "Your right arm is swollen a little. I didn't notice that last night."

"Maybe." He shrugged. "It gets some wear and tear trying to hold on to a bucking bronc."

"I'll get some ice. It'll help with the swelling." She slipped into a lightweight robe and hurried to the kitchen for a bowl of ice. In the bathroom she grabbed some towels.

After placing some ice cubes in a hand towel and twisting the ends, she straddled his back and massaged his shoulders with the ice pack until her fingers were numb. She placed the ice in a bowl on the nightstand and continued to massage his back.

"How's the rodeo circuit?" she asked.

"Good. Kinney, Watson and Hobbs are the best bareback riders in the country, and I'm finally getting numbers to match theirs."

"I'm so proud of you." She ran her hands down his back, loving the tautness of his skin, his corded muscles. "Feel better?"

"Mmm. You have angel fingers and they've awakened more urgent needs." He reached around and pulled her down beside him and quickly covered her body with his.

Later, she kissed his sleep-filled eyes. "Sleepy?"

"I sleep very little. That's when I'm weak and the nightmares take over."

"Oh, Tuf." She wrapped her arms around his neck. "You don't have to be afraid with me. I can handle the nightmares. Just don't shut me out."

He stared at her for a moment, his dark eyes guarded, and then he laid his face on her neck. "I love you." Almost instantly, he was asleep.

She stroked his hair, loving him more than she ever thought possible. "I love you, too," she whispered and vowed to help him through his fear. The only thing that frightened her was losing him.

THE NEXT DAY, TUF TOOK time to go into Billings to see a jeweler for an engagement ring for Cheyenne. He hadn't asked her yet, but they both knew it was only a matter of time. It had to be a Yogo sapphire because she loved them. He picked out a greenish-blue one and had it set in a platinum band. The ring wouldn't be ready for a couple of weeks. That was fine. He had the real thing. He had Cheyenne. Every spare moment he spent with Cheyenne and the girls. Their time alone was his little slice of heaven.

In May, Tuf and Beau were home again for a couple of days during the week. The two days passed quickly, and soon they were packing to leave again. Tuf threw his bag into his truck and noticed Ace's truck at the office. Something was up or Ace wouldn't be here this early. It was barely 5:00 a.m.

A wild neighing echoed through the ponderosa pines. What was wrong with Midnight?

He found his brother watching a computer screen.

"What's up?"

Ace glanced at him. "I'm watching Fancy Gal."

"Have you been here all night?"

"I went home for a couple of hours. Royce was here earlier. Fancy Gal's udder is tight and the foal has dropped. It could be any time or it could be later."

Tuf looked at the screen. They had webcams in the mare motel to monitor pregnant mares. Fancy Gal restlessly moved around. Suddenly she lay down in the hay.

Ace watched closely. When the mare stayed down, he leaped to his feet. "Call Flynn. Tell her to get over here... fast. And call Colt and get him to calm down that stupid horse and let Mom know what's going on."

Tuf grabbed his phone and called. His mom arrived first in her bathrobe. "What's going on?"

He pointed to the monitor.

"Oh, my."

Colt burst through the door in jeans, T-shirt and house shoes. "What the..." He saw the screen and headed to calm Midnight. "I believe that damn horse is half-human."

Flynn rushed in, her hair everywhere, carrying Emma in a carrier. She handed Tuf the baby, who was sound asleep, and ran to help Ace.

His mom was watching the screen. “Ace will take care of Fancy Gal.”

Tuf’s cell buzzed and he sat the carrier on the desk. He saw it was Austin. “Hey, Austin.”

“Tuf, I’ve been trying to reach your mom, but she doesn’t answer.”

“She’s right here. What’s up?”

“Dinah’s in labor and I’m taking her to the clinic. I wanted your mom to know.”

“I’ll tell her. We’ll be there as soon as we can.” He clicked off wondering if there was a full moon or something. “Mom, Dinah’s in labor. They’re on the way to the clinic.”

“What?” She jumped up. “I’ve got to go. I have to be there for my daughter.” She clutched her chest.

Tuf was immediately at her side. “Mom, what’s wrong?”

She took a long breath. “I’m just excited. So much is happening at once.”

Tuf wasn’t so sure. “Where’s your pills?”

“I’m fine, son.”

Uncle Josh appeared in the doorway. “What’s wrong with that damn horse?”

The agitated neighing continued.

“Fancy Gal is giving birth,” his mom explained. “And Dinah’s in labor, too. I’ve got to go.”

“I’ll drive you.”

“Make sure she has her pills, Uncle Josh.”

“Will do.”

Colt charged back in. “I can’t do anything with Midnight.”

A big, slimy blob slid out of Fancy Gal, and Tuf and Colt moved closer to the screen. Ace and Flynn knelt in the hay doing their jobs, and Tuf and Colt couldn’t see much. Ace and Flynn stood to watch the newly born black foal.

Long legs twitched and the foal raised its wobbly head. After a moment it staggered to its feet. Fancy Gal rose to her feet and licked her baby.

Suddenly the agitated neighing stopped.

Tuf and Colt looked at each other. "I told you he's part human," Colt joked.

Ace and Flynn came into the office. "Everything went fine," Ace said. "Look at that foal. All black. Not a spot on him. I think Midnight has an heir. Hey, that's not a bad name—Midnight Heir." Ace looked around. "Where's Mom?"

Tuf told him about Dinah.

"You're kidding?"

"No. I'm on my way. Just didn't want to leave Emma."

"We're right behind you," Ace replied. "What a morning."

Tuf talked to Cheyenne on the way, and thirty minutes later the whole family stood outside Dinah's door. The baby had been born ten minutes ago, and his mom and Buddy were inside getting to see their new granddaughter. Soon they were all allowed in. Austin cradled the baby in a pink blanket. Beads of perspiration peppered his forehead and his hands shook.

"Everyone, I'd like you to meet the new member of the family—Aubrey Wright." He pulled back the blanket so they could see the baby. She had swirls of damp dark hair.

"Isn't she beautiful?" Dinah said from the bed. Her hair was wet and she looked pale.

Tuf squeezed Cheyenne's hand and walked over to his sister. "Just like her mother." He kissed her forehead. "Sorry, I've got to go."

"I understand," she said. "I was raised in rodeo time."

At the door, he squatted and hugged Sadie and Sammie.

In front of everyone, he kissed Cheyenne and walked out. This time, leaving was harder than ever.

MAY PASSED IN A HAZE of roaring crowds, bucking horses and a damn buzzer that sometimes wrecked his whole day. His favorite part was going home to Cheyenne.

In June his mom made the note payment, and they celebrated with a barbecue in her backyard. The summer day was beautiful with a lot of blue sky. It seemed right and perfect sitting and holding Cheyenne's hand as they watched the girls play with Jill, Davey and Luke. Emma sat in a stroller eating Cheerios.

The girls went home with Jill and Davey to watch a movie. Buddy stayed to talk to his mom, and Tuf and Cheyenne hurried to her house to make up for the days they'd be apart.

Cowboy Christmas, a time during June and July where a cowboy could make a tremendous amount of money because of all the rodeos taking place, was about to start. Tuf wouldn't be home again until after Cheyenne Frontier Days in late July.

That night they tried to love long enough, strong enough, to make the memories last. But as he and Beau left for Reno, Tuf didn't know if he had enough strength to leave. He managed, though.

IN RENO HE CAME AWAY with a win, and he broke into the top fifteen cowboys in the country for the first time. Kinney was firmly in the number-one spot.

They crisscrossed the country rodeoing, and they met up with Ace and Colt several times when Harts supplied stock to rodeos. So far Tuf hadn't drawn Midnight and he was beginning to wonder if that was ever going to happen. In late July, they ended up in Cheyenne, Wyoming, for Cheyenne Frontier Days. Midnight was scheduled to buck, and once again Tuf didn't draw the horse on any of his rides. The cowboys that did were eager for the chance.

Beau had broken into the top fifteen bull riders, and they both knew unless something drastic happened they were going to Vegas.

This victory he planned to celebrate with Cheyenne. They drove through the night and they cruised into Roundup in the wee hours of Monday morning. He dropped Beau at the apartment above the diner. Now all Tuf wanted was to hold Cheyenne.

CHEYENNE AWOKE TO THE BUZZ of her cell. She glanced at the clock and picked it up at the same time—5:30 a.m. She had a text. I'm on my way. T

What? Tuf must have just gotten back from his rodeo trip. Jumping out of bed, she heard a light tap at the door. He was here!

Wearing pajama shorts and a tank top, she sprinted to the door and yanked it opened. Warm arms engulfed her and she melted into his embrace. Heated kisses rained on her lips, face and neck.

"I've missed you," he groaned.

"Me, too."

He wore jeans and a T-shirt and he hadn't shaved. She stroked his pronounced stubble. "Why aren't you sleeping?"

"I can't until I get my Chey-fix." His dark eyes were hooded, and she wondered if he was already half-asleep. She took his hand and led him to the sofa. They sank into the soft cushions, and he wrapped his arms around her and promptly fell asleep.

She eased out of his arms and gently put a cushion under his head. Then she lifted his boots to the sofa so he'd be more comfortable. She kissed his forehead and went to make coffee.

Her dad walked in with a frown. "Is that Tuf on our sofa?"

"Yes, crazy man hasn't had any sleep."

"When did he get here?"

"About five minutes ago. He needs some rest so let's be very quiet."

"What about the girls?" He poured a cup of coffee. "Once they see him, it'll be shouts, screams, laughs and giggles."

"I'll have to head them off. They usually wake up about six, so I have time to dress before they make an appearance." She dashed to her bedroom and quickly dressed in denim shorts and a green sleeveless knit top. Hearing little voices, she hurried to the girls' room.

"Mommy said Tuf's coming home tomorrow. Is today tomorrow?" Sammie asked her sister.

"I don't know," Sadie replied. "Let's ask her."

Before they could bolt for freedom, Cheyenne walked in and closed the door. Sammie sat in her bed. She didn't climb into Sadie's in the middle of the night anymore and she wasn't clingy. Sadie didn't run away anymore, either, and had accepted her father's death. All because of Tuf. He had made such a difference in their lives and in Cheyenne's heart. He'd made it easy to love again.

She picked up Sammie and sat on Sadie's bed. "I have a surprise."

"Tuf's here." Sadie made to jump off the bed, but Cheyenne grabbed her.

"I need you to listen. Okay?"

They nodded.

She put a finger to her lips. "We have to be very quiet."

"Why?" Sadie whispered.

"Tuf's asleep on the sofa. He's tired from rodeoing and he needs to rest."

Their mouths formed big O's.

"When will he wake up?" Sadie whispered again.

"I don't know, but we have to be very quiet so he can rest."

They put their heads together and did the whispering thing. "We can do it, Mommy," Sadie said.

Cheyenne had no doubt they could. Tuf was their hero. And hers.

She led them to the kitchen in their short cotton nightgowns. They stared at Tuf with their hands over their mouths just in case any words slipped out.

"Grandpa, Tuf's sleeping," Sadie murmured. "You have to be quiet."

Her father nodded with a smile.

She fixed cereal with a banana and juice. The girls' heads were together, and Cheyenne could hear what they were saying.

"What's Tuf gonna eat?" That was Sammie.

"He's sleeping. He can't eat, doofus."

"I'm not a doofus. You're a doofus."

Cheyenne held her finger to her lips and they started to eat. Her father got to his feet. "I'm going to the barn before I bust out laughing."

After breakfast, she herded them to their room. She dressed them in shorts and halter tops and then brushed their hair into pigtails and tied matching ribbons around them. After finding their flip-flops, she ushered them through the kitchen to the backyard. They'd made it without waking Tuf.

She sat on the porch swing as they played on their swing set. They had a small kiddie pool, which they ignored these days. Sarah's pool was much more inviting, and they often went with Jill, Davey and Luke. They were part of the Hart family, and the girls blossomed in the family environment.

School would start at the end of August. She'd enrolled them for kindergarten. Finally, they were ready to go, and Cheyenne was grateful her babies were now typical little girls. They'd gone to Billings to buy school clothes and supplies. With everything they bought, the girls had asked one question: "Will Tuf like it?" They measured everything by Tuf's opinion.

The girls sat in a swing side by side, talking. Their butts were so small they both fit. She wondered if they would always be this close. Would they always have a special language that only they understood? As they grew, would life change them? She hoped not too much. But somewhere along life's journey, she hoped to get them off pink and purple.

Tuf eased onto the swing beside her. "Hey, gorgeous."

She smiled into his dark, tired eyes. "Hey, you." She brushed the hair from his forehead. "Do you even remember coming here?"

"Some. I was tired, but I wanted to see you, and the next thing I remember is holding and kissing you. It was pretty good, too. I hope it was real."

"It was." Her hand caressed his growing beard. "I like this five-o'clock-shadow look. Sexy."

"Want me to keep it?"

"I just want you."

"Mmm. I hope we have plans for tonight." The wicked glint in his eyes caused her pulse to skitter.

"Dad's taking the girls to see their new cousin, Aubrey. They can't say her name so they call her Bre. Then they're going for supper at the diner." She kissed his cheek. "I'm so proud of you. You're one of the top bareback riders in the country."

"I have the aching muscles to prove it."

"I'll take care of that later." She winked. "Now you need to go home and get more rest so you'll be strong for tonight."

"You're teasing me."

"Yes."

He glanced toward the girls. "How long before you think they'll notice me?"

The girls sat with their legs stuck out and they were staring at the ground. Whatever they were staring at had their full attention.

"Must be a bug," she said. "They're frightened of them. It has to be a large one for them not to notice you."

"Mom…eeeek…Tuf!" Sadie leaped from the swing, quickly followed by Sammie. They jumped on Tuf, burrowing against him. For the next hour, he played with them. He swung them in the swings, played kick ball and rolled on the ground with them until all three were exhausted.

She fixed sandwiches for lunch and then put the girls down for a nap much to their protest. Tuf kissed them goodbye.

Watching him with her daughters, she knew she'd found the perfect man for them. Tuf hadn't said anything about marriage, but it was just a matter of time. Wasn't it? A seed of doubt tortured her. No. She wouldn't listen to it. Nothing could burst her bubble of happiness.

Nothing.

Chapter Fifteen

Tuf hurried home, showered, shaved and changed clothes. He thought of not shaving, but he didn't want to mar Cheyenne's skin in any way. He should sleep, but he wasn't sleepy. Letting out a long breath, he allowed himself to feel the happiness inside. It was the best feeling in the world. He had it all: the woman of his dreams, two little girls he adored, a loving family and a run for a world title. Afghanistan was finally behind him.

His mom wasn't in the house so he walked to the office. Ace and Colt were there.

Colt grabbed him and shook his hand. "Congratulations, hoss. You're sitting at number six for now. You'll inch higher since you're not through rodeoing. That's pretty damn impressive, and you're going to ride in the rodeo of your life."

Ace echoed the sentiments. "You look a little tired, though."

"I feel great." His cell beeped and he reached for it. He had a text. The ring was finally ready. Tonight he was going to ask Cheyenne to marry him.

"I've got to go." He stopped at the door. "How are the finances…in a nutshell?"

"Good." Ace nodded. "You and Beau have built up a big

sum, and come December we might make a large payment or actually be able to pay it off. Depends how well y'all do in Vegas and how much y'all put toward the ranch."

"We're paying it off. That's why Beau and I are riding so hard. And if Midnight wins the PRCA Bareback Bronc of the Year and makes it to the NFR, we can up his breeder fees."

"We're keeping our fingers crossed on that one," Ace said. "We won't know until October, but with his record we're almost certain he'll make the NFR."

"In two years." Colt held up two fingers. "We've put this struggling ranch in the black for the first time in ten years. Hell, we need to celebrate. Get drunk or something."

"Drinking is why this ranch was in a mess," Ace quipped.

Tuf knew that was a reference to their dad, but he couldn't dispute it. It was the truth. Somehow, though, it left an ache in his heart. He'd had a different relationship with their father than Ace and Colt. But above everything, they loved their father. Maybe in a different way, yet the love was still there. And they would be better men because of it.

"I've got to run. A beautiful redhead is waiting for me."

"Then what are you doing standing here?" Colt pushed him out the door.

In less than an hour he was in Billings and had the ring. He watched the blue-green Yogo sapphire sparkle. He hoped she loved it. Slipping it into a tiny velvet pouch the jeweler had given him to protect the ring, he let out a long sigh and placed it in his pocket. If he took the box in, she'd know what it was. He wanted to surprise her. This was it and he was never more ready.

He picked up red roses and a bottle of champagne and was at her house a little before four. The door was open, so he went in and stopped short. It was still daylight, but no lights were on—just candles burning on the coffee table, giving off a vanilla scent. The shades were drawn.

Cheyenne appeared in the doorway in a skimpy black negligee that showed off a lot of breast. Her red hair hung around her shoulders. His muscles tensed at her sheer beauty.

"Hey, cowboy." She walked toward him and he noticed her feet were bare—an odd thing to notice when his pulse was about to burst through his veins.

She stood on tiptoes to kiss him and his blood pressure edged up a few notches. The fragrant scent of the roses and her sexy smile blended into a beautiful picture of the evening ahead.

"If I didn't have my hands full, I'd ravage you right now."

She flipped her hair back and took the roses from him. "I'll put these in water. And thank you."

He followed her into the kitchen and held up the bottle of champagne. "Do you want this now or later?"

Settling the flowers into a vase filled with water, she shot him a teasing glance. "What do you think?"

"There's only one thing I want right now, and it's not liquor. I get high just looking at you in that skimpy thing."

Her eyes sparkled with glee. "You'll have to catch me first." She ran around the table and he followed, finally managing to corral her and swing her into his arms. With laughter and giggles smothered with heated kisses, he made his way to the bedroom and dropped her onto the bed. The laughter died away as he joined her.

The first long, drugging kiss faded into an afternoon of pleasure. Tuf fell asleep in her arms, never wanting this moment to end.

Sometime later, happiness dimmed with the sounds

of war. Gunfire blasted all around him. His buddy Frank went down.

"Tomas, I'm hit."

He fired wildly at the insurgents as he dashed toward Frank and examined him. "It's a shoulder wound."

"It hurts."

Another marine dropped down beside them and they pulled Frank behind a boulder. "Stay here. We'll pick you up on the way down."

"Tomas!"

"Stay calm. We're waiting for mortar fire." Just then all hell broke loose as a U.S. attack chopper blasted the insurgents.

"Go. Go. Go!" Tuf shouted as they charged up the hill. They reached the top and faced the enemy. "No. No. No!" There was no other way. He had to save his life and the life of his unit. "No!"

"Tuf! Tuf! Tuf!"

Someone was calling him. A woman's voice. *Cheyenne!*

He forced himself awake and found he was at the foot of the bed, covered in sweat, his muscles tight, his hands balled into fists. Cheyenne cringed against the headboard, fear in her eyes. She held one arm against her as if to protect herself. A red welt marred her upper arm.

"Oh, God. Did…did I hit you?"

She crawled toward him. "You had a nightmare and I tried to calm you."

"Oh, no, I hit you."

"It was an accident. Let me hold you. It will be okay."

"Don't touch me." He jumped from the bed and reached for his jeans. "I'm bad for you. Can't you see that?"

"No. I just see a man who's hurting."

He shoved his arms into his shirt. "I saw the look in your eyes. You were afraid."

"Yes, but only for a moment. It brought back a lot of bad memories, but I know you're not like Ryan. You would never hit me in anger."

He stopped buttoning his shirt and faced her. "There's something bad inside me, Cheyenne. It's so bad I can't even think about it in the light of day. It only comes to me in horrifying dreams. I thought happiness had freed me from them, but it hasn't. The horror is still there torturing me, and until I know what it is, there is no future for us."

"What?"

"You were right. You should have never gotten involved with another marine. I'm sorry."

Her trembling hands tucked her hair behind her ears. "You don't mean that."

"Yes, I do." He shoved his bare feet into his boots. He didn't know where his socks were and he didn't care. He had to go. He had to run.

He looked into her eyes and all he saw was the fear. "I can't risk hurting you. I will not put you through that again."

"You're hurting me now."

"I'm sorry. I'm sorry." He hit the door, running to his truck and leaving everything he'd ever wanted behind.

CHEYENNE SAT PARALYZED, and then the trembling set in. Tears soon followed. They ran down her face and onto her hands. She kept wiping them away, but more followed. It was over. Their relationship was over. Just like that. Without warning.

His tossing and turning had awakened her. Then he started screaming, flailing his arms. She tried to hold him, comfort him, but one flailing arm caught her and knocked her against the headboard. All the times Ryan had hit her and she'd tried to protect herself flooded her and she didn't know what to do. She couldn't help him, just like she couldn't help Ryan. Except Tuf hadn't hit her deliberately. But it didn't make a difference. To Tuf it was the same thing.

Her stomach cramped and she wrapped her arms around herself, feeling a pain like she'd never felt before. She eased onto the tumbled peach comforter and let the tears flow until she had no strength left. This time she knew without a doubt she would not recover. Her heart had burst open with pain, and there was no way to put it back together again.

But for her daughters she would find the strength to go on.

TUF PARKED HIS TRUCK at the house and then ran into miles and miles of Thunder Ranch land. He ran until he had no air left to breathe and then he fell to the grass and stared up at the dark sky. Thoughts and emotions warred for dominance inside him but he forced himself not to think. When he could breathe again, he slowly walked home.

Darkness engulfed him and he welcomed it, but nothing could hide the turmoil eating at him. His mother was in the kitchen and he hoped to get past her. That wasn't possible. He hadn't been able to do it as a boy, and he couldn't do it now.

"Tomas, you're home early." She turned from the sink to look at him. "What's wrong?" Her mother's instinct zeroed in on his face.

"Nothing. I'm fine." He headed for the stairs.

"Tomas…"

Voices floated up from the kitchen. "Buddy, what are you doing here…and with a gun?"

Tuf paused at the top of the stairs.

"Where's Tuf? I'm gonna kill him. He hurt Cheyenne. He hurt her bad."

"What are you talking about?"

Tuf, tired and weary, took a few steps down the stairs to face Buddy. His mom, Ace and Colt stood behind Buddy.

He held his arms wide. "Go ahead, Buddy. Fire away. I deserve it."

Before Buddy could move, his mom jerked the shotgun out of his hand. "Nobody's killing anybody. Now tell me what's going on."

"I hit Cheyenne," Tuf said loud and clear.

His mother paled. Even from where he was standing he could see that. He couldn't stop hurting people.

"What?" Buddy seemed confused. "You hit Cheyenne. She didn't tell me that."

"Yes."

"You sorry…"

"Everybody calm down." Colt stepped forward and looked up at Tuf. "You had another nightmare, didn't you? And you hit her accidently?"

"Nightmare? What are you talking about, Colton?" his mom asked.

Colt sighed. "Tuf has flashback nightmares from the war. He had one when we were on the road. In his mind he's still fighting, trying to save his men. Beau and I could hardly hold him down."

"My son is hurting and no one told me. I do not like this and I will not have my sons keeping things from me."

Ace hugged his mother. "We'll talk about this later."

"You bet we will."

"C'mon, Tuf," Colt urged. "You know it was an accident. Cheyenne knows that, too."

Austin slipped into the room. Cheyenne must have called him.

"This can be worked out." Colt kept on.

"I hit her. Do you understand that? She was scared out

of her mind, not knowing if I was going to hit her again. There's nothing acceptable about that to me. She doesn't deserve to live with someone like that, and that's all I'm saying. Now please leave me alone."

"Let's go, Dad." Austin put an arm around Buddy's shoulders, and Sarah handed Austin the gun. "What do you mean bringing a gun over here?"

"It's not loaded. I just wanted to scare him."

"You scared Sarah."

"I'm sorry, Sarah."

"Go home and take care of Cheyenne."

Buddy and Austin turned toward the kitchen. "What are we gonna tell those babies?" Buddy asked. "They worship him."

"Cheyenne will handle it, and she and Tuf will work this out."

Their voices faded as they went out the back door. He stared down at his mother and his brothers and then continued up the stairs. He paused when he was out of sight.

"Tomas, I want to talk to you."

"Mom." Ace's voice sounded stressed. "Tuf's running on empty and we need to give him some space."

"Why? He needs our love and support."

"But not right now. He has to sort this out on his own. We all know he loves Cheyenne, but he has to figure out that's all that matters. He needs time."

"My son needs me."

"Mom…"

"And why wasn't I told about these flashbacks?"

"Let's go to the kitchen and we'll talk about it."

Tuf went into his room and closed the door. He stood there feeling as though he was going to pass out from all the emotions churning in him. He backed against the wall and slid down it like a wet noodle. Drawing his knees up, he rested his forehead on them. Why was he always fighting that war? Why couldn't he wipe it from his mind?

He raised his head and stared straight ahead but saw nothing. His thoughts were inward. For the first time he forced himself to finish the dream. What was so terrifying on the top of that hill? So terrifying that it was lodged in the dark crevices of his mind, forgotten until he closed his eyes in deep sleep. What was it? All he remembered was the blasts of gunfire and then running down the hill to pick up Frank, the Afghan soldier, and check on Michael.

What was it? With the ball of his hands, he rubbed his eyes hard, but there was no answer. He was stuck in this hell that had no end.

The door opened, and Ace and Colt walked in. Colt sank down on one side of him and Ace on the other. They stretched out their legs and didn't say a word. No one spoke. It stayed that way for about fifteen minutes.

Finally, Ace said, "I can't believe Mom hasn't changed this room. It's the same as when you were twelve years old."

"Wonder if my room is the same," Colt mused. "I haven't been up here in ages."

"I'm sure Mom took down the naked women a long time ago," Ace retorted.

"Nah. She found them a week after I put them up and they're history. Your room is probably the same since you lived here until a year ago, but I bet that photo of Flynn is still hidden in your dresser."

"Nope. I took the picture with me when I moved."

The more his brothers talked, the more the pain loosened its grip.

Ace drew up his knees. "I remember how furious Dad was when you branded your furniture."

"Yeah. I was grounded for a month. I couldn't go to rodeos. That was tough."

"Did you buy the curtains and comforter?" Ace asked. "I can't remember."

"Hell, no. Mom and Dinah did that. Horseshoe sheets included."

"You still sleep on horseshoe sheets?" Colt was trying very hard not to laugh.

"Yes. What's wrong with that?"

"Davey has horses on his."

"Shut up." But from somewhere dark and deep within him where all the pain lived, a light found its way out. A light of laughter.

They laughed and it seemed so ironic for this traumatic day.

"You know, life wasn't so bad when we were kids," Colt added. "It was only later as Dad started drinking that life took a different turn, but we were still a family. Mom made sure of that."

Colt and Ace got up and each reached out a hand and pulled him to his feet.

"We're sorry you're hurting so much." Ace rubbed Tuf's shoulder. "Get some rest. You're dead on your feet. Tomorrow things will look a little better."

Colt threw an arm around Tuf. "Ace is right, and I don't say that often."

"Get some sleep," Ace said before the door closed.

Tuf fell across his bed fully clothed and with his boots on. He was so tired. He didn't have the energy to change. Sleep tugged at his eyes and he closed them, letting his mind take him wherever it wanted to go. Nothing mattered anymore.

Before the much-needed slumber claimed him, he saw Cheyenne's frightened face. It would be with him for the rest of his life.

Chapter Sixteen

The next morning, Tuf woke up still fully clothed and stiff. He hadn't moved all night and his shoulder was aching. He ripped off his clothes and took a hot shower.

He picked up his jeans to remove his wallet and loose change. He pulled out the small velvet pouch with Cheyenne's ring and his Silver Star. One was his past and the other he had hoped to be his future. He expelled a long breath. He placed the medal in the tray of buckles he'd won in his youth. The ring he slipped into his pocket, clinging to the last shred of hope he had.

To accept a future, he had to let the war go. He knew that as well as he knew his own name. And he prayed it was a possibility.

Over the next couple of days, Tuf's family gave him his space just as they had when he'd first come home. The first morning, his mom hugged him and told him she loved him, and that was it. No one pressured him. He spent that morning with his counselor going over every detail of the dream. With each dream, the details often changed, but his traumatic reaction when he reached the top of the hill was always the same.

They didn't have any breakthroughs, but at least he was talking about it. He threw himself back into rodeoing and helping out the family. They carried a load of stock for a rodeo in Great Falls, Montana, and Tuf, Beau and Colt entered to ride. Tuf and Beau wanted to maintain their ranking. After unloading and checking in, Tuf walked around talking to some of the cowboys he'd met on the circuit.

A lot of vendors were setting up near the entrance. His eyes zeroed in on red hair. *Cheyenne.* He should walk away, but he couldn't move. His eyes were glued to her face. She looked tired, worried. He'd done that to her.

Angie had a booth next to her. Luke helped his mom put out her horse cookies, and the girls chatted to Cheyenne as she arranged her jewelry and a large mirror. Buddy stood some distance away talking to someone, but he glanced at Tuf. As much as Tuf knew he should leave, he couldn't make himself do that. He couldn't tear his eyes away from her face and the sadness he saw there.

At that moment Sadie noticed him. "Tuf!"

Cheyenne's head jerked up, and all her hurt was leveled at him. The bottom of his stomach gave way and he felt sick. Sick with himself. Sick at the pain he'd caused her. And sick at life's cruel blows.

He squatted to catch the girls and held them tight as they showered him with kisses.

"Mommy's here." Sammie pointed. "She's selling jewelry and we gonna watch the rodeo." He walked them back to Cheyenne.

Angie saw them coming. "Luke, take the girls to Buddy so y'all can find a seat before the rodeo starts."

"Okay, Mom." Luke took their hands and led them toward Buddy.

Angie busied herself talking to a lady who had questions about her horse cookies. They left him and Cheyenne staring at each other with a gulf as wide as Montana between them.

She wore a short-sleeved blue blouse, and he noticed

a dark bruise at the hem of a sleeve—where he'd hit her. Tugging the sleeve lower, she tried to cover it. But it didn't work. How many times had she tried to cover bruises when she was married to Ryan? Nausea roiled in his stomach.

He fought the feeling. "How are you?"

She didn't answer. Her hand shook slightly as she rearranged her jewelry.

"I'm sor…"

"Don't say you're sorry." Her green eyes flared. "That doesn't even begin to solve anything. You want to know how I feel? I'll tell you. I feel betrayed by a man I love more than life itself. You didn't trust me enough to handle the situation. You gave up on *us*."

"I didn't give up on us. I will never do that. But you have to understand that the dreams will probably get worse and I could really hurt you. I couldn't live with that. I refuse to live with that. I have to get my head straight before I have a future to offer you. I'm not doing this intentionally. It's hurting me just as much as it's hurting you." He turned and strolled toward the chutes, feeling about as low as any man could get.

Colt met him. "What are you doing?"

"Nothing."

His brother fell in step beside him. "You hit her. It was an accident. You got to stop fighting that war in your head and let Cheyenne help you."

He stopped and faced Colt. "If I hurt her more than I already have, it would kill me. Don't you understand that?"

Colt sighed. "Aren't you already dead inside without her?"

Tuf stormed off to the chutes, but his brother was right. There was no life without Cheyenne.

CHEYENNE SHOOK SO BADLY she had to sit down.

Angie was immediately at her side. "Are you okay?"

"No," she replied. "He's hurting and I can't help him. That hurts even more."

"I'm sorry." Angie handed her a bottle of cold water.

She gulped a swallow and held on to the bottle as if it could save her. From what? She wasn't sure. Maybe from the pain.

After the encounter, Cheyenne tried to see Tuf's point of view. But all she could see was that he didn't love her enough to trust her. Luckily, she was busy and didn't have time to dwell on her shattered heart. The nights were bad. All she could think about was him.

August was big with rodeos in Montana, and she and Angie tried to make every one. She would now have two kids in school, and she would need every penny. Sometimes she would see Tuf at the rodeos, but they made no move to talk to each other. There was nothing left to say.

The next week, Cheyenne and the girls went to meet their new teacher. She thought the girls would cling to her, but they surprised her by being talkative. They sat in small chairs in Miss Huddleston's classroom. She was young and full of energy, and Cheyenne's daughters took to her immediately.

"What do you like to do?" Miss Huddleston asked them.

"We like to ride our horses," Sadie replied.

"Tuf taught us," Sammie added.

"Who's Tuf?"

Sammie was quick to answer. "He's gonna be our daddy."

"Oh."

"Our real daddy died," Sadie informed her. "We love Tuf." They both nodded their heads. Cheyenne sat in shock. She had no idea her daughters thought this. But why not? They all loved him.

It didn't stop there, though. On and on they talked about

Tuf until Cheyenne wanted to tape their mouths shut. The teacher seemed dazed because Cheyenne had told her the girls were shy and Sammie rarely talked. One of the reasons she wanted the girls to stay together instead of in different classes. They made a liar out of their mother in true fashion. She had a feeling that was going to happen a lot now that they were more outgoing and unafraid.

In September, the girls had their fifth birthday. Cheyenne had a small party at the house with Jill, Davey and Luke. Dinah and Austin came, too, with Bre. The girls showed off on their horses at the stable. As they were returning to the house, Tuf drove into the driveway.

"Tuf!" the girls screamed and raced to meet him.

"I knew you'd come," Sadie said. He pulled two large packages out of the backseat and handed them to the girls. They sat on the steps and ripped into them.

"O-oh." Sadie's mouth formed a big O. "It's beau-ti-ful. What is it?"

Cheyenne looked down at the items. "It's a horse blanket." The main color of one was purple interwoven with yellow, orange, green and brown colors. The other was pink with the same motif. On a corner their names were stitched. Cheyenne had never seen horse blankets like that. Tuf must have had them specially made and ordered months ago.

"I'm putting it on my bed," Sadie announced.

"Baby, it's for your horse." Cheyenne tried to explain it to her.

"I don't care. It's mine, not Toughie's."

"I'm keeping mine, too. It has my name on it." Sammie mimicked her sister, and they went into the house to put them on their beds.

An awkward silence stretched. No one knew what to do.

"Say hi to your niece," Dinah finally said to Tuf.

Tuf lifted the baby from his sister's arms, and Cheyenne noticed how comfortable he seemed holding four-month-old Aubrey. He would make a wonderful father if only he'd allow himself that honor.

Tuf left soon after and they hadn't even spoken. They were at least twelve feet apart at all times. She wanted to reach out and touch him, feel the heat of his skin against hers. She wanted it so badly she hurt.

Life would be easier if they didn't see each other all the time, but they were connected by family and that wasn't possible. Back in July when it was clear Tuf and Beau were going to make it to the finals in Vegas, Sarah had booked a block of rooms for the family and Cheyenne, the girls and Buddy.

She couldn't change her plans now because it would hurt Sarah's feelings, and Cheyenne had wanted to sell her jewelry at the Western-themed Cowboy Christmas Gift Show at Las Vegas Convention Center for years. Over four hundred vendors from the U.S. and Canada would be there to sell their wares from jewelry to Western apparel. It was a great opportunity for her. She and Angie had already booked spaces.

Angie wasn't a fan of rodeos, but Duke wanted to see Tuf and Beau ride in Vegas, so she'd agreed to go. Everyone supported each other. That's what families did. But Cheyenne didn't feel like a part of the Hart family, and she and Tuf would always be twelve feet apart.

TUF RODEOED IN MONTANA, his region, and stayed close to home to help carry stock to rodeos. His points in the standings changed with each rodeo, and he ended up in fourth place behind Kinney, Watson and Hobbs. The odds of him beating them in Vegas were very slim, but he kept in shape, preparing for the biggest rodeo of his life.

In October, the Hart family received the news they'd been praying for. The Midnight Express had been voted by the cowboys as the PRCA Bareback Bronc of the Year. Ace bought a case of champagne, and the family held a party at the house. After years of struggle, his mother's dream had come to fruition. Her decision to diversify into raising rodeo stock had been risky, but she saw it as a way to save the ranch she loved, and her instincts had been right. The Harts were in the rodeo contracting business—big-time.

Colt raised his glass. "C'mon, Ace. Say it one more time. Colt was right."

Ace clinked his glass against Colt's. "Hell, yeah. Colt was right."

Leah stood by Tuf watching her husband. "In about ten minutes, my husband is going to be drunk on his ass with happiness."

"He's done an amazing job with Midnight this year."

"Yeah. Everyone has done an amazing job to pull this ranch out of debt, including you." She kissed his cheek. "Don't forget to be happy." He felt she wanted to say much more, but stopped herself.

After everyone had left, Tuf stood in the kitchen with his mom.

"I didn't see you drink a thing."

"My mind's already messed up. I don't need liquor."

"Tomas, I would rather be in debt for the rest of my life than to see you so unhappy."

"I know, Mom." He kissed her forehead. "Night."

He went upstairs to his room and stood at his window, looking toward the Wright property.

And dreamed of Cheyenne. All he had now were his dreams…and his nightmares. Which one would win the battle in his head?

IN NOVEMBER, THE HARTS were busy trying to finalize plans for Vegas—not only for the family, but for the animals. Besides Midnight, Bushwhacker, Back Bender, Asteroid, Bossy Lady and True Grit had been invited to the big show.

After going over details many times, a final plan emerged. Tuf, Duke, Colt and Leah would transport the animals. The rest of the family would fly out. Because of Dinah's job, she and Austin didn't make the trip. Jill and Davey didn't, either. They stayed with Leah's mother. Leah decided to go with the stock to share the experience with Colt and to take care of the paperwork once they arrived.

Over Thanksgiving, they went over the plans again. Tuf wondered if they'd ever leave. With the cattle carrier, the drive would take from seventeen to nineteen hours depending on stops to water the stocks, and bathroom and eat stops for them. They would drive through the night. Tuf followed the carrier in his truck in case they broke down and so they'd have a vehicle in Vegas.

They left Thunder Ranch about noon and arrived in Las Vegas at six the next morning. Midnight was in the TV pen, which contained champion horses that were fun to watch, and he would buck on nights five and ten of the ten-day event. His breeding fee was now a hot commodity.

While Colt and Leah dealt with paperwork, Tuf and Duke drove the small distance to the Thomas and Mack Center on the University of Nevada Las Vegas campus. The football-like stadium was awesome.

"Are you nervous?" Duke asked.

"Hell, yeah." Even though he was numb inside, he felt a flicker of nerves.

Duke slapped him on the back. "You'll do fine."

They joined Colt and Leah. The animals had made the trip without a problem. Midnight, on the other hand, was restlessly circling the pen, wanting out.

Later the family arrived, and after settling in, they had dinner together. Cheyenne, Angie, Duke and Luke were taking the cookies and jewelry they'd had shipped over to the convention center to find their spaces and figure out what else they had to do. He should be helping Cheyenne. But he sat missing her and wondering if his pain would ever end.

The girls and Buddy joined them. Sadie and Sammie squeezed in next to him, and after picking at their food, they crawled into his lap. He held them tight, drawing strength from their warm little bodies.

I have to let the war go drummed through his head. For a life with Cheyenne and the girls, he had to let the war go. He just wasn't sure how to do that. God knew he'd tried so many times, but the bad stuff was still there inside him like a festering sore that would not heal.

Maybe he was always going to be trapped between good and evil.

THE NIGHT BEFORE THE RODEO started, his mom, Ace and Colt attended an awards banquet to receive the PRCA World Champion Award for Midnight.

The National Finals Rodeo started with a big fanfare. The stadium was packed and the tension level high as the cowboys readied for the biggest night of their lives. The crowd stood as Reba McEntire sang the national anthem. Tuf and Beau sat on their horses, loaned to them by a rodeo friend, with their hands over their hearts. Whooping and hollering, the cowboys and cowgirls charged out into the arena in their Wrangler National Finals jackets and took off their hats to the crowd. The roar was deafening.

Sadie and Sammie stood at a rail, waving. Buddy had a hand on each one. "Tuf!" they screamed, and he tipped his hat to them. They went back to their seats with the rest of the family.

Bareback riding was first. In the locker room, Tuf donned his protective vest, chaps and spurs and made his way to a platform where the cowboys could watch the action.

"This is it, Tuf," Cory Kinney said. "Good luck." They shook hands as friends who wanted the same thing but only one could win.

Chad Canter from Stillwater, Oklahoma, was up first. All eyes were on the chutes as Chad burst out on Foxy Lady. He made the ride to the roar of the crowd and scored an 87. That set the bar high and the next ten cowboys didn't beat it. Neither did Jesse Hobbs. Tuf was up next. He settled onto Fire and Ice, his draw, a chestnut-colored mare.

"Just stay calm," Colt said as he helped Tuf adjust his rigging. The owner of the horse attached the flank strap, and the horse moved restlessly, ready to buck.

"She bucks hot and cold," the owner said. "Just be ready for the hot, 'cause she'll bust your ass."

"Thanks," Tuf said, fitting his hand into the handle.

The announcer's voice came on. "Up next is Tuf Hart out of Roundup, Montana. He's the youngest of the Hart rodeo family. His father rodeoed, as do his brothers, Ace and Colt, and his cousins Beau and Duke Adams. This is Tuf's first full year on the circuit and it's been a banner year for him. A former marine, you might notice his red, white and blue garb. This guy is cowboy tough. Let's see what he can do here tonight on Fire and Ice, owned by Barker Rodeo Company of Denver, Colorado."

Tuf raised his left arm, leaned slightly back and stretched out his legs, ready to mark the horse before her front hooves hit the ground. He took a deep breath and shut out everything but him and the horse. He nodded to the gate handler to signal he was ready. The gate swung open with a bang, and Fire and Ice bolted out bucking with a powerful force. Tuf held on, keeping his rhythm marking the horse. Four. Five. The horse kicked high with her back legs, trying to dislodge him. He managed to stay on. Seven. Eight. The buzzer shrilled and Tuf let go, sailing to the ground and losing his hat. The congratulation whoops and clapping were deafening, and the bright lights blinded him for a moment. Picking up his hat, he stared at the JumboTron. Waiting and waiting.

The ride was good, he assured himself. Seemed like forever before 88.5 popped up. He started to throw his hat into the air when he heard his favorite squeaky little voices shout, "Tuf!"

He tipped his hat to his munchkins and they stopped screaming. Buddy had a death grip on them and guided them back to their seats. Tuf walked out of the arena and joined the other cowboys to watch the last two riders. Beau joined him.

"Good ride," Beau said.

"Yeah. Let's see if it holds up."

It did. No one bested his score in the first round.

Winning the first round gave him a boost. He'd earned money for Thunder Ranch, but his arm and his heart ached, and he wondered if he could withstand nine more grueling nights without seeing Cheyenne.

Chapter Seventeen

Cheyenne didn't have time to think about Tuf, but she got updates from the family, her dad and the girls. She'd wanted to share this experience with him. Once again, though, they were so far apart.

She and Angie had been over almost every inch of the 300,000 square feet of the North Halls Las Vegas Convention Center. The place was jam-packed with every Western item imaginable from furniture to art to handcrafted items. They had fun browsing through the treasures.

Most of the time they were at their booths selling their wares. Her leather-and-turquoise cuff was the most popular item. She feared she'd run out before the show ended. Angie was busy, too. People had a lot of questions about her cookies and what was in them. They passed out tons of business cards.

But her thoughts were over at the Thomas and Mack Center. Tuf had won the first round and she wondered how he felt about that. He had to be happy about it.

The girls and Luke sat on the floor behind them playing with a deck of cards.

A lady tried on a silver necklace with a horseshoe pendant. "I like this. It's very simple. I'll take it."

Cheyenne swiped the woman's card and put the necklace in one of her trademark brown boxes with an orange *C* on top.

Josh Adams, Earl McKinley and Buddy walked up, and the kids ran to them. Earl pushed Emma in a stroller and the girls kissed her cheeks. "Bye," the kids shouted and followed their grandfathers through the mill of people to the door.

Angie stared at her.

"What?"

"Go over and watch Tuf ride. He wants you there."

"No, he doesn't."

"Cheyenne…"

Her words were cut off as Leah, Flynn, Sierra, Jordan and Sarah strolled over.

"How's business?" Leah asked.

"Good."

They checked out the jewelry and talked for a minute.

"We better go." Jordan spoke up. "Joshua is waiting at the entrance."

"Yes. I don't want to miss Tomas ride." Sarah glanced at her watch.

"Why don't you come for a little while?" Sierra suggested to Cheyenne.

"Thanks, but no."

"It's fast-paced and exciting until someone you love gets on a two-thousand-pound angry bull. I don't have any fingernails left and it's just the beginning."

"You'll survive," Flynn said. "I better find my daughter."

Her friends left, but Leah lingered. "Please go to the arena and watch Tuf ride."

"Thanks, Leah, but I can't."

"You two take stubborn to a whole new level."

"It's Tuf… I…"

"I know. He's so sad. I just want to hug and slap him at the same time."

"That's the problem. He's shutting everyone out, even me. If he'd just let me help him, I'd be over there cheering him on."

"If you change your mind, just call me."

"I won't. I can handle a lot of things, but I can't handle Tuf not trusting me enough to understand and share his pain."

A group of women came up, and Leah waved and left. As the women tried on pieces, she wondered why Tuf couldn't love her enough.

THE SECOND NIGHT, CORY won on Black Widow. Trey Watson won the third round. It was going to be a dogfight to the bitter end. Adrenaline surged through Tuf's veins and he settled in to compete for the next seven nights.

The fourth night, Jesse Hobbs won. The fifth night, Tuf scored an 88.5 on Wild Deuce. Cory drew Midnight.

"Ladies and gentlemen, next up is Cory Kinney out of Hutto, Texas. He's number one in the standings and he's riding The Midnight Express. This stallion's lineage dates back to Five Minutes to Midnight, a hall-of-fame bucking bronc a lot of old-timers will remember. The stud has made it to the NFR five times and was chosen the NFR bucking bronc two times. He disappeared from the rodeo scene for a while until the Hart family purchased him at auction. He's had a great year winning the PRCA bucking bronc of the year in October. This is Midnight's sixth appearance at the NFR. Let's see what he and Cory Kinney can do tonight."

Midnight kicked and bucked but Cory stayed on. Tuf held his breath, waiting for the score.

When 89 came up, Beau muttered under his breath, "Shit."

Midnight was magnificent, though. Every bareback rider there wanted a chance at the stallion because they knew the stud had the power to garnish a top score that could lead them to the world title.

Cory won again on the sixth night with an 88.5 ride on Razzle-Dazzle. Tuf placed second again.

Beau suited up for his ride. He was feeling the frustration, too. He'd garnered second and third spots but hadn't won a round yet.

"I want to win a round, Tuf," Beau said as he put on his helmet. "That's where the money is."

"You have a good chance since only one out of eleven cowboys have managed a ride this round."

"I drew Hellacious Sam and he's a mean bastard. He'll trample you if he gets a chance."

"Show him who's boss, coz. Good luck." Tuf ran back to the rail to watch. Duke joined him.

"He can win this round," Duke said.

"Yep. Let's watch."

The chute gate flew open, and Sam fired out like a bullet bucking with a surge of power. Beau held on. The bull went into a spin. Still Beau held on. The buzzer blared and Beau jumped off, landing on his backside.

"He did it," Duke shouted and they high-fived.

But Sam wasn't through. He turned and charged before Beau could get out of the way. With one thrust of his powerful head, Sam threw Beau into the air, and Beau landed on his back with a thud. Sam stood over him, stomping around, daring anyone to take his prize.

The clowns and cowboys on horseback tried to get Sam away from Beau to no avail. Sam swung snot six ways from Sunday and was ready to take them on.

"Shit." Tuf jumped over the rail, followed by Duke. Their appearance startled Sam, and the clowns were able to get in and distract him. The bull charged the clowns, and the handlers had Sam headed toward the open chute in a split second.

Tuff fell down by Beau in the dirt. "Beau!"

"It hurts," Beau moaned.

A flashback from Afghanistan hit Tuf like a sledgehammer. No! He would not keep fighting that war. That was in the past. This was the present. And Beau was not Frank.

"Where?" Duke asked as Tuf checked Beau's dust-covered body.

"My…my left arm. I can't move it."

Damn. It was probably broken. Tuf realized there was complete quiet in the large stadium. The announcer wasn't even talking as they waited for news on Beau's condition.

"What do you think?" Duke asked.

"Probably best to get a stretcher," Tuf replied.

"No." Beau vetoed that. "Sierra has to see me get up. Just help me."

"Don't be stupid." Duke wasn't having any of it. "That bull gave you a tromping."

Beau turned to Tuf. "Help me up."

"C'mon, Duke, it's what he wants. Support his arm while I help him."

Beau bent his knees, and Tuf put his hands beneath Beau's shoulders and lifted while Duke raised Beau's arm and held it against his chest.

"Shit. It hurts. What's my score?" Beau said all in one breath.

"Look up," Tuf told him.

Beau glanced at the JumboTron. "Hot damn. Eighty-nine."

A cowboy retrieved Beau's hat, and Tuf stuffed it on Beau's head as they made their way out of the arena through the cowboys to a ramp to the locker room. The crowd erupted with loud applause. Colt and Ace met them there, as did the rodeo doctor.

While Beau was being x-rayed, Tuf hurried to get his truck because he feared Beau's forearm was broken. It had an S shape. The bull had obviously stepped on it. And he knew Beau was going to fight getting an ambulance every step of the way.

Tuf's fears were confirmed, and they got him to the hospital as quickly as possible. Sierra, Uncle Josh and Jordan were meeting them there. Beau was quiet on the ride to the hospital. Everyone was.

They took Beau in right away and prepped him to get the bone set. Sierra arrived in time to see him before they whisked him away. The rest of the family trickled in and they waited. Sierra came out with tears in her eyes.

"I'm so sad for him. He knew the cowboys here were good and he's placed every night, but he wanted to win at least one round."

Everyone seemed to reach for his or her phone at the same time. They'd been so worried about Beau they hadn't checked to see how the bull riding had come out.

Colt was fastest on the draw. He gave a thumbs-up sign as he talked. "He won," Colt shouted. "Only two cowboys made their rides, so Beau's gonna get a big payout on this one."

"Oh, that's good news," Sierra cried. "I can't wait to tell him."

The doctor decided to keep Beau until morning and Sierra stayed with him. Tuf promised to pick them up in the morning.

At ten the next morning, Tuf's cell woke him. In less than five minutes, he was dressed and headed for the door.

Ace met him in the hall. "Give me your keys. I can collect Sierra and Beau. You need your rest. You have to ride tonight."

"I gave my word and I'm going."

"You got a thing about giving your word, and it's nice to be so honorable, but I didn't see any of that when you ditched Cheyenne."

Tuf frowned at his brother, who was usually so calm and rational. Was he goading him? "I didn't ditch her. I broke up with her to protect her."

"Mmm." Ace nodded. "Or are you protecting yourself?"

"What?"

"Cheyenne's been through her own kind of hell with an abusive husband. She knows what being hit for real feels like. Yet, when you had the nightmare, she was willing to accept you warts and all, but you're the one who backed out of the relationship. Why? Because you have one foot in that war at all times. It controls you. During the day you're good at protecting yourself from all those memories. At night there is no protection and the memories torture you. You have to stop protecting whatever bad stuff's in your head. Let it out, please, and start to live again."

Tuf stared at Ace as if he'd grown two heads. Was he that transparent?

TUF HAD BEAU AND SIERRA back at the hotel in no time. Beau looked a little pale, but he seemed okay. He lay in bed and Sierra propped pillows behind his back.

Their affection for one another got to Tuf. Cheyenne would be upset if he was hurt, too. *Because she loves me.* He closed his eyes briefly to let that sink in. Was Ace right?

Was he protecting himself? Protecting the awful memories? And how did he stop? He didn't know how to stop.

He couldn't think about this now. He pulled up a chair to sit by the bed. "How are you?" he asked.

"Sore and mad," Beau replied.

"I'm sorry your NFR experience ended like this."

"Yeah. This broken arm sucks, and I wish I could have walked out of the arena under my own steam after the win, but, man, I'm going home with over sixty thousand dollars. I'm happy about that." Beau scooted up in bed. "The damn bull stunk and he peed on me."

"He marked his territory," Tuf quipped.

They laughed and Tuf got to his feet. "I'll catch y'all later. Right now I'm going to crash for a few hours."

When Tuf reached his room, he stripped out of his clothes and fell across his bed. But visions of Cheyenne tortured him. He'd crushed something valuable—her love. And he had to make it right. This wasn't the time or the place, though. Now he had to concentrate on the rodeo and his commitment to his family.

That night Tuf won the round on Magic Realm, and Trey won the eighth round. That left two nights, and Tuf would have to win both to win the title. The pressure was on, and it was the buzz around the cowboys. Could Tuf come from behind to win? Or could Trey? Could Cory maintain his lead? Who was going to win?

On the ninth night, Cory made his ride with an 88.5. Tuf had to beat that to stay in contention. He drew Scarlet Lady, a horse known to buck hard and wild. As he slid onto the reddish-colored mare, the horse immediately tried to jump out of the chute, banging against the pipe. Tuf got off and a man from Pioneer Rodeo who owned the horse tried to calm her.

Tuf eased onto Scarlet one more time.

The announcer's voice came on. "Let's turn our attention to chute number three. Tuf Hart is ready to ride."

Tuf took a deep breath and shut out everything but himself and the spirited horse beneath him. He nodded and the gate swung open. Scarlet leaped out of the gate. Bucking, leaping and kicking, Scarlet showed no mercy. Tuf settled into a hard, rocking rhythm. Five, six. Tuf held on. A wild kick from Scarlet's back legs almost unseated him, but Tuf managed to stay on. Seven. Eight.

At the buzzer, Tuf jumped off, lost his balance and staggered backward. And backward until his head hit something and the arena went black.

Home to Thunder Ranch in a coffin. He saw the coffin clearly draped in an American flag. Saw his mother crying. Saw Cheyenne…Cheyenne! No! He forced his eyes open and saw the people in the stadium, waiting.

"Tuf!" he heard his munchkins scream.

Colt and Ace ran toward him, and Tuf lumbered to his feet. The arena swayed as thunderous applause erupted. He blinked, trying to focus, and waved to the girls to let them know he was fine.

"Are you okay?" Ace asked as he reached him.

"Yeah. Just lost my balance."

"Look at the score," Colt shouted, handing him his hat.

Tuf looked up to see 89 stuck on the JumboTron as if it was waiting for him to notice it. He lifted a fist in the air in acknowledgment and walked out of the arena with his brothers flanking him.

"The cowboy marine is walking away," the announcer said. "He's tough. Congratulations! Tuf Hart wins the round on Scarlet Lady. This sets the stage for a showdown between Tuf and Cory Kinney. It'll be a nail-biter, so don't miss bareback riding tomorrow night when we crown a champion. Now get ready for more excitement…"

The voice faded away as they walked up the ramp to the locker room. Tuf sank onto a bench and took off his spurs. Ace felt Tuf's head, his neck and his shoulders.

Tuf pulled away. "Will you stop? I'm not a horse you can practice your vet skills on."

"There's a knot on the back of your head where you hit the advertisement sign. You might have a concussion."

"I can handle it."

"Yeah, you're a tough-ass," Ace snapped. "You can handle everything by yourself."

Cowboys walked in and out. Several shouted, "Way to go, Tuf. Good ride." He lifted a hand in response.

Colt knelt in front of him. "Why are you so down? You've worked all year for this and broke into the top fifteen cowboys in the country. You're standing toe-to-toe with the best riders in the world and you have a chance to win it all. Every cowboy here wants to be in your boots. Why aren't you two-stepping across this room in joy?"

"Because I made a mistake with Cheyenne and I keep making them."

"Tuf, we all make mistakes. Why do you think I didn't see my son until a year ago? I wanted to, but I thought he was better off without me. Big mistake. Give Cheyenne a chance. It won't be a mistake."

Tuf stood, as did Colt. He removed his chaps and protective vest and placed them in his locker. "I need some time alone."

"Tuf. . . ."

He walked away. He was good at that.

CHEYENNE SANK ONTO THE BED as she and Angie returned from another day at the convention center.

"Why does love hurt so much?"

Angie sat by her. "I don't know. Sometimes it just does.

Life's about changes, accepting, forgiving and moving on. I feel your situation with Tuf can be resolved with a simple 'I'm sorry' from Tuf."

Cheyenne shook her head. "No, it can't. Tuf doesn't trust me enough to handle his nightmares. That's not going to change. He said he's been having them for over two years and they could get more violent. There's no way around that."

"Unless Tuf lets you into his thoughts."

Cheyenne looked at her friend. "That's not going to happen and…"

The buzz of her cell interrupted Cheyenne. She rummaged in her purse for it. "It's a text from Leah."

"What does it say?" Angie asked.

Cheyenne couldn't speak. She kept staring at the words.

"Cheyenne…?"

She read the text word for word because she couldn't form any of her own. "'Tuf got hurt. He hit his head on a sign, but he's okay. Just thought you'd want to know.'"

Tuf is hurt.

Chapter Eighteen

Cheyenne's first instinct was to run to the arena, but Tuf had made it very clear he didn't need her comfort or anything else. She hated the ache inside that she couldn't control.

"Cheyenne?"

She turned to her friend. "What?"

"Are you going to the arena?"

"No. He hasn't asked for me."

Angie rolled her eyes. "You need an invitation?"

"Oh, no. The girls are there, and they probably saw what happened." She called her dad and he answered promptly. "How are the girls?"

"Fine. Why?"

"Leah said Tuf got hurt."

"Yeah, but they just thought it was part of the rodeo. They were screaming 'Tuf, get up' so loud they put them on the large JumboTron. They saw themselves and waved and screamed louder. Tuf waved to them and they were fine. They're waiting for barrel racing. That's their favorite next to Tuf riding. Since Beau was injured, they don't want to watch those mean old bulls, so we'll be back after barrel racing."

"Okay. Thanks, Dad."

She dropped her phone into her purse. Tuf was fine. That was all that mattered.

TUF MADE HIS WAY OUT of the arena and started walking. Then he broke into a run like he always did when the walls closed in and he tried to escape the pain inside himself. Through the pounding of his heart, he realized he had to stop running. With extreme effort, he made himself stop, and then he just kept walking. He had no destination in mind, but he wound up back at the hotel. He took the elevator up to his room.

Cheyenne's room was next to his, and he paused outside her door. He had to see her. He didn't care about anything else. For the first time in his life, he needed someone. He couldn't handle life without Cheyenne. After admitting that, he felt better. They could talk and work this out—if only she'd forgive him.

He knocked and waited, but there was no response. She had to be out. That was no problem. He'd wait in his room until he heard her come in. All the days they'd been in Vegas, not once had they run into each other. When he woke up, she was already at the convention center. When he came in from the rodeo, she and the girls were asleep.

Sitting in his room, he listened for a noise next door. He had acute hearing. Something he'd mastered in Afghanistan. The hallway was relatively quiet, though. He could call Cheyenne, but he needed to see her.

His cell beeped with a text message. It was from Michael Dobbins. Good luck, buddy. Rooting for you all the way. M

Tuf sat staring at his phone and realized the war was always going to be a part of him. He'd made lifelong friends, and he and Michael had a special connection—a bond that could never be broken. All along he'd been thinking if he could get rid of the bad memories, he could live life again. But it wasn't like that at all. He had to find a way to live with the memories, and he could only do that with Cheyenne. It was so clear now. He couldn't fight the memories alone.

A tap at the door had him on his feet. Maybe it was Cheyenne. His mother stood outside. "Hi, son. How do you feel?"

"I'm fine." He opened the door and she came inside. Her hands went immediately to his head. "Oh, you do have a knot. Does it hurt?"

"Nah," he lied.

"We've decided to take in a Reba McEntire show and then have dinner. Would you like to come?"

"Who's 'we'?"

"Earl, Buddy and me. Everyone else is spending this last evening with their spouses, and we thought we'd have some fun, too. Tomorrow night we'll be busy packing, getting ready to catch a flight home."

"No, but have a good time."

"I plan to. Now I'm going to change and put on some sparkly earrings I bought from Cheyenne." She paused. "You do know her room is next door."

"Yes, Mom."

She hugged him. "I'm so proud of you. Win or lose tomorrow, you're our hero."

The word didn't bother him like it usually did. "Thanks, Mom. Have a fun evening."

After she left, he took off his boots, planning to stay in and order dinner. He didn't want to leave the room in case he missed Cheyenne.

His right arm ached so he took two Advil and lay across the bed. Listening. Waiting.

Thirty minutes later, he felt drowsy and he fought it, but soon sleep claimed him.

THE NEXT MORNING, IT WAS almost noon when he woke up. Damn it! He jumped up, slipped into jeans and yanked a T-shirt over his head. He hurried to the hallway and knocked on Cheyenne's door, but he knew she was already gone. Slowly, he went back to his room. Sitting on the bed, he slipped on his boots. He had to find Cheyenne.

Thirty minutes later, he found her. A group of women gathered around her booth trying on earrings, bracelets and necklaces. She was busy and he couldn't talk to her in front of a crowd. But he watched her for a moment to get himself through the day. Her hair was up like he'd seen so many times. He'd take it down just to run his fingers through the silky strands and to kiss the warmth of her neck. The taste of her skin was strong on his lips. He turned and walked away. A habit he was beginning to hate.

Back at the hotel, he took a hot shower to ease his aching muscles. The knot on his head had gone down, so that was good. Before long, he headed over to the arena. He was anxious to get his draw for the night. The horse he'd have to ride would play a big part in his chance for a title.

He stood with the other fourteen cowboys to get their draw. Tuf was stunned, hardly believing that his year had come down to this.

"Who'd you draw?" Cory asked.

"Midnight."

"Well, now, my odds just got a little better."

"Maybe."

"I hope we can still be friends after this," Cory said.

"I don't see why not. We'll buddy up anytime we can." Tuf walked off to where his brothers stood.

"Who'd you get?" Colt asked.

"Midnight."

"You're shitting me."

"Nope. I got the black stallion."

"Damn," Ace said. "What a finale. Just stay focused. You can ride him."

"Yeah. You've been a little distracted, but now you really have to rein in your emotions," Colt added.

"I gotta go. It's time to ride in." Reining in his emotions might be the hardest thing he'd ever have to do, and that included riding Midnight.

In the locker room, Tuf strapped on his chaps and grabbed his Wrangler NFR jacket out of his bag. As he slipped it on, Beau walked in, his arm in a sling.

"You riding in?" Tuf asked.

"You bet. This is the last night and I'm not gonna miss it." He held up his arm in a cast. "I'm not putting on my jacket. Do you think anyone will mind?"

"Nah. Let's saddle up." They headed toward the pens where two horses were waiting. Because of the brace, Beau had to mount from the right side. The horse didn't seem to mind. They got in line behind other cowboys waiting to ride into the arena. A cowgirl carrying the U.S. flag rode in on a beautiful golden palomino. The lights dimmed and a spotlight shone on the girl as a starlet from Vegas sang the national anthem. He bowed his head and placed his hand over his heart. When the last note died away, the bright lights came on, and the cowboys and cowgirls charged into the arena single file for the last night of the rodeo.

The pace was fast as they circled the arena and then lined up side by side. The crowd roared with applause. Tuf and Beau came to a stop in front of where the Hart family sat. Sadie and Sammie were at the rail waving. Tuf nudged his horse forward and tipped his hat to them.

"Tuf!" they screamed.

He backed his horse into the lineup and saw they were captured on the big screen.

"Show-off." Beau laughed.

Soon they charged out of the arena whooping and hollering. A sense of excitement filled the air. Nine long days, and tonight world champions would be awarded in each event. Time to rodeo. Time to find out who those champions would be.

TUF SAT IN THE LOCKER ROOM attaching his spurs, mentally preparing himself.

"This is it," Beau said. "This is what we've worked for all year, sleeping in the truck, eating crappy food. It's all come down to a hell of a ride."

Was this what he'd worked for? In his mind that didn't seem right. And he knew what it was. All year he'd worked to regain his freedom. Freedom from the nightmares. Freedom to live again—with Cheyenne. But he hadn't accomplished that. He took a long breath and suddenly realized that freedom was a state of mind. And his mind was locked in combat.

The past nine nights hadn't been the thrilling experience he'd expected and he knew why. Cheyenne wasn't here. But for his family, he would do his best.

He placed his hand over his jeans pocket and felt the ring he carried. Cheyenne's engagement ring. Then it hit him. He couldn't ride tonight without her here. It was that simple. He jumped to his feet.

"Where you going?" Beau asked.

"I have to see Cheyenne."

"What? Bareback riding is fixing to start. Are you nuts?"

"I have to see her."

Beau shook his head.

"Cover for me with Colt and Ace. I'll be back."

"You better be."

Tuf made his way out of the cowboy-ready area and

then broke into a run. His spurs jangled, but he didn't have time to take them off. A shuttle was outside letting people off to see the rodeo. He jumped on and did something his pride wouldn't let him do last night.

He called Cheyenne.

CHEYENNE AND ANGIE WAITED for the elevator.

"It's over. After ten long days, I sold out of horse cookies and I'm ready to go home."

"Me, too," Cheyenne said. "Although I do have a few earrings left, but I plan to give those to some of the ladies here in the hotel."

"That's nice."

Cheyenne's cell buzzed and she fished it out of her purse. *Tuf.* Her heart raced as she read the name.

"Where are you?" he asked quickly.

"Uh…at the elevator in the hotel. Why?"

"I need to see you. Can you meet me at the entrance?"

"Why?"

"Please, Cheyenne. Just for a minute."

The *please* got her. "O-okay."

"Who was it?" Angie asked.

"Tuf. He wants me to meet him outside."

"What are you waiting for?"

"You're coming with me. I'm not standing out there alone. There are a lot of strange people here."

"Like my one-hundred-and-ten-pound frame is going to deter anyone."

"You know what I mean." Cheyenne's hand shook as she dropped her phone into her purse. *What does Tuf want?*

"Yeah. Let's go." They walked toward the entrance. "Bareback riding is first, isn't it?"

"Yes, and I don't know what Tuf is doing coming here. He should be getting ready to ride."

They went through the glass doors and into the cool evening. People were milling around, laughing and talking.

A man puffing on a cigarette sidled up to them. "Hey, ladies, need a little company?"

"No, thanks," Cheyenne replied.

"You sure?" The cigarette bobbed on his lip. "I could show you gals a good time."

"Will you get that smoke out of our faces?" Angie said in a voice Cheyenne had never heard her use before. As the man turned tail and went back into the hotel, Angie laughed. "Hey, guess I'm tougher than I thought."

Cars and cabs dropped off people, but she didn't see any sign of Tuf. Then a shuttle bus roared up and Tuf jumped out dressed in his red, white and blue rodeo garb, including the spurs that jangled as he rushed toward her. At the sight of him, her heart knocked wildly.

"Hey, cowboy, lost your horse?" a guy shouted at him, but Tuf ignored him, running straight to her.

"Listen, Cheyenne, I screwed up. I know that now. I'm sorry, but please come to the rodeo and watch me ride. If you love me, if you think we have a future, you'll be there. I need you to be there."

Hurt feelings and love warred inside her. "But you don't need me. You've proven that in the last few months. You shut me out and refused to trust me. And 'I'm sorry' doesn't even start to erase all that pain."

He cupped her face, and she felt the calluses on his hands. "If you love me, none of that will matter. Be there—for us. I've got to go." He ran and leaped on the shuttle that was waiting for him, and it roared away. For some reason, she felt as if he'd stomped on her heart, and she couldn't get past that feeling.

"Why didn't you go with him?" Angie asked.

"What?"

"You should have gone with him on the shuttle."

"I can't."

"Cheyenne."

"I just can't."

"Then why are you crying?"

"I'm not crying." She brushed away tears with the back of her hand, belying her statement.

"Your face is leaking, then."

"Angie, it's not that easy. We still have the same problem. He doesn't trust me."

"This whole week you kept saying he hasn't asked you. Now he has. It's time to go."

"It's not that simple."

"Oh, but it is. I'm getting a cab. I'll even go with you, and you know I don't like rodeos." Angie turned toward the curb.

"No, don't."

"Cheyenne." Angie stomped her foot.

"Please understand I can't do this. I'll talk to him later when we have more time."

"By then it will be too late. The rodeo will be over and you'll regret your decision."

Cheyenne drew a heavy breath and looked at the sparkling lights of Vegas that rivaled a thousand Christmas trees. People passed by her as if she didn't exist, and in a way she felt all alone battling the pain inside herself.

"Don't do this to yourself." Angie kept up her pleas.

"I can't seem to do anything else."

Angie hugged her. "I'm sorry."

"Me, too."

TUF MADE IT BACK INTO the cowboy-ready area amid a few startled stares. Luckily none of them were Colt's, Ace's or Duke's. He thought he was home free until Ace stalked up to him.

"Where in the hell have you been? I've looked all over. Beau said you were in the bathroom. Are you sick?"

"No. I…"

"You're not a kid anymore, Tuf. What…"

Suddenly, without warning, the part of his brain he'd kept vaulted tight opened and he could see what was on the top of that hill—the horror. The unthinkable horror he'd protected for years. He staggered backward with the force of the truth. Ace caught him and he struggled to regain his composure.

"Damn, you are sick," Ace said. "I'm sorry. I shouldn't have yelled at you."

"I'm fine." He sucked in puffs of air and stood on his own two feet.

"You don't look fine. You're pale and shaky."

Before Tuf could reply, Duke ran to them. "Kinney just scored a 90 on Tempting Fate."

"Shit." Ace shook his head.

"Colt has Midnight in the chute, Tuf. You ready?" Duke asked.

Two sets of eyes stared at him. A year of riding the circuit had come down to this moment. His stomach was raw, his back tight and his nerves frayed, but he ignored all that and said, "Yes."

He walked to the chute, but before climbing it, he put his hand over his right pocket and felt the ring. *She'll come. She'll come.* Climbing the chute, he kept repeating that.

He carefully slid onto Midnight's back, and the stallion flung his head in protest. Beneath him, Tuf felt the raw power of the animal. It was like sticking his finger in an electrical socket and knowing he was going to get knocked for a loop. Strong muscles rippled, and Midnight banged restlessly against the chute, ready to buck.

The announcer's voice came on. "Ladies and gents, Cory Kinney just made an outstanding ride. Tuf Hart is getting ready and he has to be feeling the pressure. Everyone is. Bareback riding has come down to this last ride. This is as exciting as it gets."

Ace and Duke helped with his rigging, and Colt worked with Midnight's flank strap. He was the only one who did that on Midnight. As soon as Colt tightened it, Midnight jerked his head.

Tuf slipped his gloved right hand into the handle on the rigging and worked his hand to get a secure grip.

"You about ready?" Ace asked.

"Is Cheyenne sitting with the family?"

"What?"

"Look and see if Cheyenne is with the family."

"Tuf, forget about Cheyenne for a minute."

"Look, damn it."

Ace raised his head. "No, she's not there, but the twins are waiting."

The bottom dropped out of his stomach, and he fought to regain his focus. For his family, he had to focus.

He got into his groove.

"Good luck," Ace and Duke shouted.

Then Colt was there. "You know how Midnight bucks. Just be prepared for the power."

The announcer's voice pushed through. "In chute number two, Tuf Hart is on The Midnight Express, owned by the Hart family. This horse has the power to get the job done, and Tuf Hart knows it. As does everyone here. For Tuf the trick will be to stay on the horse for eight seconds. What do you think, Bob?"

The other announcer chimed in. "Cory Kinney had an

impressive ride and it's going to be hard to beat that. But anything can happen here. Tuf Hart's got the talent, though. Let's see what happens."

Everything faded away, and it was just him and Midnight. And eight seconds. He raised his left arm and nodded. The gate banged open, and Midnight reared up on his hind legs out of the chute, almost unseating Tuf, but he kept his balance and his grip. And the show was on. The power of the bucks jarred his kidneys, strained his back and his arm, and pounding waves of pain shot through his head, but he got into a rhythm and kept it. He lost track of the count and thought the damn buzzer must be broken. It felt as if the black stallion had jarred his body for at least ten minutes. Then he heard it and let go. The power catapulted him into the dirt and he landed on his back. Pain radiated through his body. He thought he was dead, but if he was, he wouldn't be able to feel the agony.

He stared up into the bright lights and thought he should get up, but he couldn't move a muscle.

The announcer's voice penetrated the fog. "Cory Kinney is waiting for the score to pop up. Everyone is. I'm glad I don't have to judge this, Hal. That was an astounding ride. Man, what an ending to bareback riding."

"Wait, Bob. Tuf Hart is not getting up. Is he hurt?"

"Ace and Colt Hart and Duke Adams are racing to his side. Big Ben, the clown, is there, too. Everyone is waiting for this tough cowboy marine to get to his feet. I'm sure the Hart family is holding their breath."

Tuf stared at a big red nose.

Then there was Ace's, Colt's and Duke's anxious faces. "Tuf, you okay?" Ace asked.

"I might need a hand up."

With a smile, Ace and Duke lifted him to his feet.

"What's my score?" Tuf asked.

"It hasn't come up yet," Colt replied. "I don't know what's taking so damn long."

The crowd erupted into applause and shouts. "There it is," Duke pointed.

"Hey, hoss, look at that," Colt shouted. "Congratulations, bro. I have to check on Midnight."

Tuf glanced up and saw 91. He'd done it. He'd won the title. But where was his joy?

"C'mon, Tuf, show some reaction." Ace slapped him on the back. "The crowd expects it."

"You might have to lift my arms."

Ace laughed, and there in front of eighteen thousand people, his big brother hugged him. "I'm proud of you. Dad would be, too."

"Thanks." Tuf picked up his hat.

"Tuf Hart seems a little dazed," Hal said. "I don't think he realizes he just won the title."

"Tuf!" The little voices drew Tuf's attention. He lifted his hat in acknowledgment, trying not to flinch, and froze. Cheyenne stood with them, her hands over her mouth in worry.

She's here.

Renewed adrenaline pumped through his veins, recharging his tired and sore body.

"Tuf, where you going?" Ace shouted.

"Where's he going, Hal?"

"He's climbing into the stands where those little red-haired girls have been cheering for him all week. And now there's a young red-haired woman there."

Tuf swung over the rail at Cheyenne's feet. "I love you," he said to her startled face. He pulled the ring out of his pocket. "Will you marry me? Nightmares and all."

"Tuf." Her eyes glistened with tears.

"Yes or no?"

"Y-yes." She hiccuped.

He slipped the ring onto her finger and kissed her, and suddenly he was at peace for the first time in a long, long time.

"Tuf," she whispered against his lips, "people are clapping and staring at us."

He drew back and saw all eyes were on them. "Let's get out of here." But he couldn't move for the two munchkins wrapped around his legs. He knelt down. "Stay with Grandpa. I love you."

"I love you, too," they called as Cheyenne and Tuf made their getaway to the roar of the crowd.

The announcer's voice followed them. "Congratulations to Tuf and his special lady."

"Tuf Hart is our bareback-riding champion. This cowboy marine has had a big night."

TUF PULLED CHEYENNE into a corner away from the bathrooms and people milling in and out of the stadium.

"You came. You came," he said, stroking her hair and kissing her briefly.

"I didn't want to," she admitted. "I fully intended not to. I was hurt and 'I'm sorry' just didn't cut it, but in the elevator I couldn't stop crying and realized that no matter how much you hurt me I still loved you. The next thing I knew, Angie and I were in a cab coming here." She sighed and leaned her head against his chest. "We still have the same problem, Tuf. This hasn't solved anything."

He lifted her chin from his chest. "Everything's changed. I now know I can't handle the nightmares alone. I need you. I need your love and support."

"Oh, Tuf..."

"And there's more. When I snuck back into the cowboy-ready area after seeing you, Ace was livid and said something like I wasn't a kid anymore. Suddenly the steel curtain across my brain lifted and I could see what happened on the top of that hill in Afghanistan. The scene that was too horrible to recall."

"What was it?"

He cupped her face so he could look into her green eyes. "When we got to the top, six insurgents were coming out of a cave with high-powered weapons. We took them out, as ordered. Only after we shot them did we realize they were just boys. Maybe fourteen, fifteen years old. We killed kids."

"Oh, Tuf." She wrapped her arms around his neck and held him. "It was either you or them and it was war."

"I know, but I have such a hard time with that—so hard that I blocked it from my mind for over two years. It has controlled my life, my thoughts and my dreams, but not anymore. I'm ready to live again, to love and be happy with you and the girls. I'm not saying the nightmares are over. They will probably always be a part of me, but I give you my word as a marine, as a cowboy, I will never shut you out again. And you know if I'm known for anything, it's keeping my word. We'll work through it together."

She kissed the side of his face. "That's all I ever wanted." She drew back and looked at the ring on her finger. "I love the Yogo sapphire. It's gorgeous. I've never seen one quite this color. Look how it catches the light."

"I told the jeweler I wanted it as close to green as possible to match your eyes."

"It's perfect." She raised her eyes to his. "I love you."

He gathered her into his arms again and held her. "I love you, too, and that's never going to change."

"Congratulations, cowboy. I'm so proud of you," she whispered into his neck. "Don't you have to go back to the rodeo?"

"Probably." He stepped back and held out his arms. "Look at me. I'm happy. I'm free."

She burrowed against him. "Yes, you are. I am, too."

He reached for her hand. "Later, we'll get reacquainted."

She laughed softly and his heart soared. Amid all the pain, he truly had found happiness. Arm in arm, they made their way back into the stadium so Tuf could be awarded his gold buckle. But he'd already won what he'd really wanted.

Cheyenne.

Epilogue

Christmas morning

"Are they awake?" Sammie asked.

"I don't know," Sadie replied. "I can't see. It's dark."

"Mommy said not to get up early. We're gonna get in trouble."

"Nobody gets in trouble on Christmas."

Tuf ran his hand across his wife's bare stomach. "The munchkins are awake."

"I hear them," Cheyenne replied, kissing his shoulder. "I guess we better get up."

"Yep." He reached for his robe.

The early moonlight spilled through the window, and Tuf glanced around his horseshoe bedroom. Never in a million years did he ever think he'd have Cheyenne Wright in his bed, much less make love to her until after midnight. It seemed surreal at times, but wondrous and uplifting, too.

So much had happened since Vegas. They were married that last night of the rodeo in a small chapel surrounded by the whole family.

Once the ceremony was over, Sadie had asked the minister, "Are they married?"

The man looked a little confused, but answered, "Yes."

"Is Tuf our daddy now?" Sadie had quizzed Cheyenne.

"Yes, baby." They did the twin-talk whispering thing, and from that moment on they called him Daddy. It sounded right and it felt right. In the New Year, he planned to hire a lawyer to adopt them. He and Cheyenne had talked about it. They would keep Sundell as their middle names.

When they'd returned from Vegas, they'd stayed at the Wright house, but it was crowded. There was no place for his clothes in Cheyenne's jewelry-supply-cluttered room. He slept there and ate there but showered and changed at his mom's until Cheyenne could make room. He even looked at mobile homes to solve the problem, then his mother had stepped in. She wanted them to move into the house. She said they could have the upstairs because she never went up there unless she was forced to.

Tuf wasn't sure how the family would feel about that, so he called a family meeting. Ace said he and Flynn were happy at the McKinley place and he had no problem with the arrangement. Neither did Colt and Leah, who had house plans already drawn up and were starting construction soon. Beau had plans to fix up the foreman's house for him and Sierra, and Duke and Angie had their own place. That left Dinah. She surprised them by saying she had no desire to live in her childhood home. She and Austin wanted to build a home one day either on the Wright property or at Thunder Ranch. Because of his mother's heart condition, they all felt better that someone would be in the house with Sarah. No one had enough nerve to tell her that, though.

So he, Cheyenne and the girls had moved in for now, but Tuf laid down some rules. His mother was not to be their maid. She would not cook for them, clean or pick up after them. So far it was working out.

They had left the girls' furniture at Buddy's for when they visited. Cheyenne wanted the twins to have separate rooms, but so far that wasn't working. They slept in Dinah's old room. Cheyenne planned to do some redecorating after the first of the year, but now they intended to enjoy the holiday with the family.

He flipped on the light and yanked the door wider. "What are you two doing?"

The girls jumped back, their green eyes wide. "You scared us, Daddy," Sammie said, and they flew into his arms. "It's Christmas. It's Christmas!"

Cheyenne joined them in her green robe, yawning with a video camera in her hand. "What time is it?"

"Five."

"Let's go, Mommy. We have to see if Santa's been here." The girls darted down the stairs.

"Wait a minute," Cheyenne called. "We don't want to wake Grandma Sarah."

They crept down the stairs through the foyer and started toward the great room when his mom and Buddy appeared from the kitchen.

"Grandma Sarah's awake," Sadie shouted. "And Grandpa's here, too."

"I wouldn't miss my girls' Christmas." Buddy hugged his granddaughters.

Tuf turned on the light, and the girls' mouths formed big O's at the brightly colored packages under the ten-foot spruce tree. Scents of pine, vanilla and cinnamon filled the room. A roaring fire in the fireplace enclosed them in cozy warmth. Snow silently fell outside the French doors.

They sat on the sofa and watched as the girls tore into their gifts. Cheyenne filmed away, and they laughed at the girls' excitement.

Tuf scooted closer to his wife. "Happy?"

"Yes."

He brushed her hair from her face. "I love you."

She nuzzled into him, resting her head on his shoulder. "Mmm. I've never been this happy. Ever."

"Me, neither." Whatever they had to face down the road, he knew they could handle it. Cheyenne now went with him to see the counselor so she could learn more about helping him. He didn't have a problem with that. Admitting he needed help was his first step in healing. He hadn't had any more nightmares, but if he did, he was prepared to handle that, too—with Cheyenne. He wasn't afraid to go to sleep, either. Finally, he had found his peace with the woman of his dreams.

It wasn't long before the family started arriving. Joshua and Jordan arrived first, quickly followed by Dinah, Austin and Bre. The others slowly trickled in. Colt and Leah were last because they had to pick up Evan. Sarah and Cheyenne had made enough food to feed an army, and everyone thoroughly enjoyed it. They did the white-elephant gift exchange, which caused a lot of laughter and family rivalry. The kids exchanged gifts, and the adults sat back and enjoyed Sarah's spicy cider.

After they sang Christmas carols, Sarah got to her feet. "I don't want to give a long speech, but I have to say how proud I am of all of you. We accomplished an awful lot this year, not because of one person, but because we worked together as a team, as a family. There were times we all wanted to kill that black stallion, but he came through for us. We have the PRCA horse of the year and NFR horse of the year. Midnight's breeder fee has gone up. Not only that, Bushwhacker placed second at the NFR. Another great accomplishment. Our breeder program continues to improve with great stock that will become champions, especially Midnight Heir. Our program is now recognized by everyone in the country. The Harts of the rodeo are in business and out of debt." She reached for some papers on the coffee table. "Thanks to everyone's effort, our note is now paid in full."

"Hot damn," Colt said. "A happy ending."

"It's not an ending, son," his mother told him. "As Tuf once said, it's the beginning. We're almost booked solid for next year, and we have a long list of owners wanting to breed their mares to Midnight."

"It's all good news, Mom," Ace said.

"And the lease on the three thousand acres is up for renewal next year. I've decided to take our land back and to continue to build our bucking program. We will have plenty of room to do that." She turned and tossed the papers into the fireplace. Everyone clapped.

"I just want to say one more thing. I'm so happy my youngest is home safe. For eight years I went to bed every night wondering if I'd ever see my son again." Her voice cracked.

No, Mom. Don't do this.

He got to his feet but she waved him back. "Of all the accomplishments this year, Tuf's happiness has been at the forefront of my mind. I'm so grateful he and Cheyenne have found each other. My heart is full. I love you all." She reached for her glass on the coffee table. "Let's make a toast."

Duke and Beau got to their feet. "I..." they said together and then stopped when they realized the other was speaking.

"Go ahead," Duke said.

"No. You go ahead," Beau replied.

"We'll have to flip a coin." Colt intervened, digging in his pocket. "Man, this is reminiscent of our childhood.

You two doing everything at the same time." He flipped a quarter in the air. "Call it."

"Heads," Duke said before Beau could.

Colt looked at the coin on the floor. "Heads it is. Duke, what do you have to say?"

"Can I tell, Daddy?" Luke asked.

"Sure, son." Angie curved into Duke's side, and Duke had a hand on Luke's shoulder.

"I'm gonna get a little baby brother or sister," Luke said, his little chest puffed out.

Everyone jumped up in joy.

"Wait a minute," Beau said. "I didn't get my chance."

Everyone sat down again.

"Sierra and I are expecting, too."

"You're kidding." Colt started laughing loudly. "You guys synchronize everything."

"Behave," Leah said.

"Wait. Wait. Duke, when's the baby due?" Colt asked.

"August tenth."

"Beau?"

"August eighth."

"This is hilarious." Leah gave Colt a narrow-eyed glance and he added quickly, "But great."

Everyone hugged and added their congratulations to the two couples.

"Jordan, we're going to have two more grandbabies in August," Uncle Josh declared, beaming from ear to ear.

"Yes, and Sierra didn't mention a word."

Sierra hugged her aunt. "We wanted to surprise you."

"You certainly did that."

"What a wonderful Christmas," his mom said. "Any more exciting news?" She glanced around the room.

"Don't look at us, Mom," Colt said. "We have four kids, and one of them has four legs."

"You're hopeless." Leah kissed Colt's cheek.

"Same goes for us." Ace put his arm around Flynn. "We have one and that's enough for now."

Dinah sat in Austin's lap. "Our baby is finally sleeping through the night, so don't even think of looking our way."

"And we just got married." Tuf made that clear, but he couldn't imagine anything making him happier than having a child with Cheyenne.

"Get your glasses," his mom said. "I want to make another toast."

When everyone had a glass, Sarah raised hers. "To wise decisions, Midnight and the rodeo. May the Harts and the Adamses continue to prosper and grow—as a family in Roundup, Montana."

Tuf wrapped his arm around Cheyenne and whispered, "Merry Christmas."

"Merry Christmas."

At the love in her eyes, he knew he had what he'd been fighting for—freedom to live again with a girl he'd loved since he was a boy.

He was finally home.

* * * * *

COMING NEXT MONTH
from Harlequin® American Romance®

AVAILABLE JANUARY 2, 2013

#1433 A CALLAHAN OUTLAW'S TWINS

Callahan Cowboys

Tina Leonard

When Kendall Phillips announces she is pregnant with Sloan Callahan's twin sons, the loner ex-military man realizes he has to change his outlaw ways...and start thinking of a way to propose!

#1434 REMEMBER ME, COWBOY

Coffee Creek, Montana

C.J. Carmichael

An accident left Corb Lambert with amnesia and he can't remember Laurel Sheridan, let alone getting her pregnant. Will a hasty marriage solve these problems—or make them worse?

#1435 THE SEAL'S VALENTINE

Operation: Family

Laura Marie Altom

Navy SEAL Tristan Bartoni's heart was broken when his wife left him and took their son. So how can he be attracted to Brynn Langtoine and risk his heart again for her and her cute kids?

#1436 HER RANCHER HERO

Saddlers Prairie

Ann Roth

Cody Naylor fosters four troubled boys on Hope Ranch. Is it appropriate that Cody is falling for his new housekeeper? Will her leaving at the end of the summer throw the boys into turmoil? Or just Cody?

Turn the page for a preview of

THE OTHER SIDE OF US

by

Sarah Mayberry,

coming January 2013
from Harlequin® Superromance®.

PLUS, exciting changes are in the works!
Enjoy the same great stories in a longer format
and new look—beginning January 2013!

HSREXPINTRO2012

Coming January 2013

THE OTHER SIDE OF US
A brand-new novel
from Harlequin® Superromance® author
Sarah Mayberry

In recovery from a serious accident, Mackenzie Williams is beating all the doctors' predictions. But she needs single-minded focus. She doesn't *need the distraction of neighbors—especially good-looking ones like Oliver Garrett!*

MACKENZIE BREATHED DEEPLY to recover from the workout. She'd pushed herself too far but she wanted to accelerate her rehabilitation. Still, she needed to lie down to combat the nausea and shaking muscles.

There was a knock on the front door. Who on earth would be visiting her on a Thursday morning? Probably a cold-calling salesperson.

She answered, but her pithy rejection died before she'd formed the first words.

The man on her doorstep was definitely not a cold caller. Nothing about this man was cold, from the auburn of his wavy hair to his brown eyes to his sensual mouth. Nothing cold about those broad shoulders, flat belly and lean hips, either.

"Hey," he said in a shiver-inducing baritone. "I'm Oliver Garrett. I moved in next door." His smile was so warm and vibrant it was almost offensive.

"Mackenzie Williams." Oh, no. Her legs were starting to

HSREXP1212HH

tremble, indicating they wouldn't hold up long. Any second now she would embarrass herself in front of this complete and very good-looking stranger.

"It's been years since I was down here." He seemed to settle in for a chat. "It doesn't look as though—"

"I have to go." Her stomach rolled as she shut the door. The last thing she registered was the look of shock on Oliver's face at her abrupt dismissal.

And somehow she knew their neighborly relations would be a lot cooler now.

Will Mackenzie be able to make it up to Oliver for her rude introduction?
Find out in THE OTHER SIDE OF US by Sarah Mayberry, available January 2013 from Harlequin® Superromance®. PLUS, exciting changes are in the works! Enjoy the same great stories in a longer format and new look—beginning January 2013!

HSREXP1212HH